He grinned. "So, how was the outing after the task force meeting?"

"Good," she said. "I bought a copy of your book."

"Really?" He lifted a brow.

"Yes, and read the entire thing in one sitting," Paula admitted, at the risk of giving him a big head. "It was quite interesting in giving a deeper perspective on criminal profiling."

"Glad you were able to pick up something from it," Neil said, wiping perspiration from his brow with the back of his hand. "You never know how much will register and how much won't."

"It registered," she assured him. "As did what you had to say during the task force meeting."

"Good." He grinned sideways. "I really do want to help in any way I can to bring this unsub to justice. Or at least give you more to work with in delving into his psyche as a serial killer."

She nodded. "You're succeeding on both fronts."

T0120474

In memory of my beloved mother, Marjah Aljean, a devoted lifelong fan of Harlequin romance novels, who inspired me to excel in my personal and professional lives. To H. Loraine, the true love of my life and best friend, whose support has been unwavering through the many terrific years together; and Carole Ann Jones, who left an impact on me with her amazing talents on the screen; as well as the loyal fans of my romance, mystery, suspense and thriller fiction published over the years. Lastly, a nod goes out to my great editors, Allison Lyons and Denise Zaza, for the wonderful opportunity to lend my literary voice and creative spirit to the Harlequin Intrigue line.

CAMPUS KILLER

R. BARRI FLOWERS

Harlequin

INTRIGUE

If you purchased this book without a cover you should be aware that this book is stolen property. It was reported as "unsold and destroyed" to the publisher, and neither the author nor the publisher has received any payment for this "stripped book."

Harlequin®
INTRIGUE™

ISBN-13: 978-1-335-45683-0

Campus Killer

Copyright © 2024 by R. Barri Flowers

Recycling programs for this product may not exist in your area.

All rights reserved. No part of this book may be used or reproduced in any manner whatsoever without written permission.

Without limiting the author's and publisher's exclusive rights, any unauthorized use of this publication to train generative artificial intelligence (AI) technologies is expressly prohibited.

This is a work of fiction. Names, characters, places and incidents are either the product of the author's imagination or are used fictitiously. Any resemblance to actual persons, living or dead, businesses, companies, events or locales is entirely coincidental.

For questions and comments about the quality of this book, please contact us at CustomerService@Harlequin.com.

TM and ® are trademarks of Harlequin Enterprises ULC.

Harlequin Enterprises ULC
22 Adelaide St. West, 41st Floor
Toronto, Ontario M5H 4E3, Canada
www.Harlequin.com

Printed in Lithuania

MIX
Paper | Supporting responsible forestry
FSC® C021394
www.fsc.org

R. Barri Flowers is an award-winning author of crime, thriller, mystery and romance fiction featuring three-dimensional protagonists, riveting plots, unexpected twists and turns, and heart-pounding climaxes. With an expertise in true crime, serial killers and characterizing dangerous offenders, he is perfectly suited for the Harlequin Intrigue line. Chemistry and conflict between the hero and heroine, attention to detail and incorporating the very latest advances in criminal investigations are the cornerstones of his romantic suspense fiction. Discover more on popular social networks and Wikipedia.

Books by R. Barri Flowers

Harlequin Intrigue

The Lynleys of Law Enforcement

Special Agent Witness
Christmas Lights Killer
Murder in the Blue Ridge Mountains
Cold Murder in Kolton Lake
Campus Killer

Hawaii CI

The Big Island Killer
Captured on Kauai
Honolulu Cold Homicide
Danger on Maui
Chasing the Violet Killer

Visit the Author Profile page at Harlequin.com.

CAST OF CHARACTERS

Paula Lynley—A detective sergeant at Addison University's Department of Police and Public Safety, in Rendall Cove, Michigan, she is investigating a string of suffocation murders of female professors. She enlists a criminal profiler to help crack the case and finds herself drawn to the handsome ATF special agent.

Neil Ramirez—A visiting criminologist, he uses his expertise on violent offenders to assist the beautiful detective while gathering intel on a suspected local arms trafficking operation. Could the cases be connected? When Paula becomes a target of a serial killer, Neil is determined to keep her out of harm's way.

Gayle Yamasaki—An investigator for the Rendall Cove Police Department's Detective Bureau, she is working the Campus Killer case and feels the pressure to solve it before there are more victims.

Michael Davenport—A campus police detective, he is committed to tracking down the serial killer, whatever it takes.

Craig Eckart—A local arms trafficker under investigation. But could he also be doing double duty as a campus serial killer?

The Campus Killer—A cunning and determined serial murderer of attractive female professors, who deviates from the norm when going after Paula for the kill.

Prologue

Debra Newton loved being a journalism associate professor in the College of Communication Arts and Sciences at Addison University in the bustling college town of Rendall Cove, Michigan. In many ways, it was truly a dream come true for her, having graduated from the very school a decade earlier. Now she got to teach others, inspiring young minds for the formidable challenges of tomorrow. And with the summer session well underway, she was doing just that, putting her journalistic skills to the test with each and every passing day.

She only wished her love life could be nearly as thought-provoking and satisfying. Bradford Newton, her college sweetheart turned husband, had turned out to be a total jerk, with a roving eye that went after anyone wearing a skirt at his law office. After one time too many of being played for a fool, she finally kicked him to the curb five years ago, and Debra only wished she had done it sooner. Since her divorce, she had just dated occasionally, with most men seemingly less interested in her brain and sense of humor than her flaming long, wavy red hair, good looks and shapely physique. While these various sides to her were important in and of themselves, she wanted to be seen as the total package and wanted the same in a partner.

Which was why she had turned down a date with a handsome and persistent colleague who, though also single, was a little—make that a lot—too full of himself and a bit scary at times in his demeanor. Similarly, a former administrator, who on paper checked a lot of the boxes for what she was looking for in a potential mate, did not measure up in practice and real time, forcing her to reject his half-hearted advances.

As if that wasn't almost enough to turn her off of romance for good, there was the fact that one of Debra's students had become fixated on her to the point of stalking. Though she had made it abundantly clear that she would never even consider dating a student—not even one who was nearly her own age, having been a late bloomer as an undergrad—this one didn't seem to take no for an answer. She had decided that enough was enough. She would bring it up to the director of the School of Journalism, as well as report it to the campus police, for the record.

After classes were over, Debra hopped into her black Audi S3 sedan and headed home. Peeking into the rearview mirror, she could have sworn that she was being followed by a dark SUV. Was her imagination playing tricks on her? Maybe she was getting paranoid for no reason, brought on by her musings.

This apparently was the case, as the vehicle in question veered off onto another street, the driver seemingly oblivious to her imaginative thoughts. Much less, out to get her. Relaxing, Debra drove to her apartment complex just outside the college campus on Frandor Lane, parked in her assigned spot and headed across the attractively landscaped grounds. She climbed the stairs to her building's second-floor two-bedroom, two-bath unit. Inside, she put down her mini hobo bag with papers to grade, kicked off mule loafers and strode barefoot across the maple hardwood flooring to the galley kitchen. She took a bottle of red wine from the refrigerator, poured herself a glass and considered if she should eat in or go out for dinner.

While still contemplating, Debra bypassed the contemporary furnishings and took the wineglass with her to the main bedroom. *Maybe I'll just have a pizza delivered,* she told herself, while removing the hairpin holding her bun in place, allowing her locks to fall free across her shoulders.

Then she heard the sound of a familiar voice say almost comically, "I was beginning to think you'd never get here, Deb."

The unexpected visitor's words gave Debra a start, causing her to drop the glass of wine, its contents spilling onto the brown carpeted floor. He was standing in her bedroom as if he owned the place. How did he get inside her apartment? What did he want?

"When I sensed that you might be on to me as I followed your car, I took a shortcut to beat you here, while giving you a false sense of security."

She recalled the SUV that had been following her and then seemingly wasn't. Why hadn't she remembered the type of vehicle he drove?

"Sorry about the wine," he said tonelessly, glancing at it and the glass on the floor. "At least you managed to have a sip or two. As for what's probably foremost on your mind, honestly, it wasn't all that difficult to break into your apartment. It has a relatively cheap lock that's easy to pick for someone who knows what he's doing."

Debra froze like an ice sculpture while weighing her options, then asked him tentatively, "What do you want?" Was he actually going to rape her to get what he wanted? Then what? Leave her alone to forever remember what he did? Or report it to the police and have him arrested and charged with a sex crime?

Why couldn't he have simply put the moves on someone else who may have been interested in his advances? Or did he get his kicks from power tripping by forcing the action? No matter how she sliced it, Debra didn't like the outcome. Maybe she could outrun him and escape the apartment, wherein she could whip the cell phone out of the back pocket of her chino pants and call for help. Except for the fact that he was now standing between her and the exit from the room.

"It's not good for you, I'm afraid." His voice burst into her thoughts, while taking on an ominous octave. "You need to die, and I'm here to make sure it happens."

As her heart skipped a few beats in digesting his harrowing words, this was when Debra knew she had to make her move before it was too late. What move should that be? The answer was obvious. Anything that could get her out of this alive. And, hopefully, not too badly injured.

HE ANTICIPATED THAT she would try to hit him where it hurt, easily blocking her futile efforts. He was also way ahead of her next instinct to try to somehow worm her way around his sturdy frame and escape what was to be a veritable death trap. He caught her narrow shoulders and tossed her toward the platform bed, expecting her to fall onto the comforter. But she somehow managed to stay on her feet and was about to scream her pretty head off, alerting neighbors. He couldn't let that happen.

It only took one well-placed hard blow to her jaw to send Professor Debra Newton reeling backward and flat onto the bed, where she went out like a light. Now it was time for him to finish what he started. She had no one to blame but herself for the unfortunate predicament she was now in. They were all alike when it came right down to it. Believing they could screw guys like him over and not be held accountable. Wrong.

Dead wrong.

He lifted the decorative throw pillow off the bed and, just as she began to stir, placed it over her face, pressing down firmly. Though she struggled mightily to break free, he was stronger, far more determined and, as such, took away her means to breathe air before she lost her will to resist altogether and became deathly still. When he finally removed the pillow, he saw that her blue eyes were wide open, but any life in them had gone away for good.

He sucked in a deep breath and tossed the pillow back on the bed beside her corpse, pleased with what he had done to the professor and already looking ahead for an encore. After all, she wasn't the only one who needed to be taught a lesson that only female educators could truly appreciate. He laughed at his own sick sense of humor before vacating the premises and making sure he was successful in avoiding detection while engineering his masterful escape.

IT WASN'T LONG before he picked up right where he'd left off. Again and again. Now yet another one bit the dust. Or, if not quite ashes to ashes, dust to dust, the good-looking professor was very much dead. He had seen to that, watching as the life drained out of her like soapy water in a tub. She had been expecting someone else, apparently. But got him instead. Her loss. His gain.

Like the ones that came before her, he did what he needed to do. What they forced him to do, more or less. Suffocation was such a tough way to die. Fighting for air and finding it in short supply when being cut off from the brain was challenging, to say the least. But that was their tough luck. He made no apologies for playing the villain, falling prey to his inner demons. The ones that drove him to kill and get a charge out of it when the deed was done.

He took one final look at the dead professor and imagined her looking back at him, had her eyes not been shut for good. Maybe she would meet up in the afterlife with the others and form a dead professors' society or something to that effect. He nearly burst into laughter at the devious thought but suppressed this, so as not to alert anyone of his presence.

Leaving the scene of the crime, he made his way down the back stairs, and like a thief—make that murderer— in the night, he moved briskly away from the building without looking back. Only when he was in the safety of his car and on the road did he allow himself to suck in a deep and glorious breath, knowing that he had escaped successfully and could go on with his life as though he hadn't just committed another cold-blooded murder that, like those before her, she never saw coming.

Not till it was much, much too late.

Chapter One

"Looks like the Campus Killer has taken another professor's life." The words lodged deep in Detective Sergeant Paula Lynley's throat like a jagged chicken bone stuck there, as she relayed this depressing information over speakerphone to Captain Shailene McNamara, her immediate superior in the Investigative Division of the Department of Police and Public Safety at Addison University. Paula was behind the wheel in her duty vehicle, a white Ford Mustang Mach-E, en route to the crime scene, the office of Honors College Associate Professor Odette Furillo.

Shailene made a grunting sound. "That's not what I wanted to hear to start my day."

You and me both, Paula told herself, in total agreement on a Wednesday at 9:00 a.m. Unfortunately, there was no getting around this, painful as it was for both of them to digest. "Ms. Furillo was apparently working late. Her body was discovered by a student this morning," Paula informed the captain, implying that it didn't appear to be an active crime situation to prompt a shelter-in-place order. "All signs seem to indicate that the victim was suffocated to death."

At least this was what Paula was led to believe by the first responder to the scene, Detective Michael Davenport, one of the investigators under her command in the AU DPPS. If true, this would mark the fourth suffocation-style murder of an Addison University female professor on or close to the campus in Rendall Cove over the past few months. The first came during the early part of the summer session, when a thirty-three-year-old associate professor in the School of Journalism, Debra Newton, was found asphyxiated to death in her apartment. And a month later, thirty-four-year-old Department of Horticulture Assistant Professor Harmeet Fernández was discovered dead in the Horticulture Gardens.

Near the end of the summer session, thirty-six-year-old Kathy Payne, a professor in the College of Veterinary Medicine, was fatally suffocated in her residence. Now, just a couple of weeks into the fall session, Paula had to consider the very distinct possibility that a fourth professor had been murdered in a similar manner by the so-called "Campus Killer," the moniker the unsub was given by the press. If so, that would leave little doubt that they were dealing with a bona fide and devious serial killer on and around the campus, where there had been an increase in patrols after the first professor was murdered near the university. Apart from a general belief that they were likely dealing with a male perpetrator—based on the nature of the crimes and circumstantial evidence—as of now, there had been no identifiable DNA or fingerprints to point the blame at anyone in particular. And no reliable surveillance video that could give them a clue about the unsub. Nor had any of the suspects panned out thus far. Would it be any different this time around?

The ongoing case was being jointly investigated by the Rendall Cove Police Department, considering that the first and third murders linked to the killer had occurred off campus, within the Rendall Cove city limits. Paula hoped that they would be able to soon crack the case with the latest purported homicide at the hands of the unsub. "Of course, we won't know anything for certain on this front till the autopsy is completed," she told her, as if Shailene wasn't aware of this.

The captain responded tersely, "I get that. Keep me posted on the developments in this disturbing investigation."

"I will," Paula promised as always, before disconnecting. She sighed, feeling just as disturbed that they were involved with this type of crisis in what was normally a peaceful, beautifully landscaped campus environment, split by the Cedar River, with countless imposing trees, lush green spaces, winding paths and newly renovated buildings. But someone had chosen to threaten that tranquility in the worst way possible.

While keeping her bold brown eyes on the lookout for bicyclers, who at times recklessly believed they owned the roads, Paula's thoughts slipped to her personal trials and tribulations over the past eighteen months. At thirty-five, she was a year removed from her divorce from Scott Lynley. The veteran FBI special agent had once been the love of her life. It was a love that seemed destined to last forever. But somewhere along the way, things fizzled between them and, once it became apparent that no magical elixir would fix them, they decided it would be best to go their separate ways. For Paula, an African American, an interracial marriage was never a problem to her. A clash of strong wills between her and Scott, however, proved to be a major issue.

Deciding she needed a clean break, she relocated from Kentucky to Central Michigan, where in a lateral transfer, Paula landed an opening with the Addison University PD. Equipped with a Bachelor of Science in Criminal Justice and a minor in Law, Justice and Public Policy from the University of Louisville, where she excelled and was a member of a sorority, she welcomed the opportunity to return to a campus atmosphere for police work. But now it was being put to a major test, and it was one she fully intended to pass at the end of the day.

Same was true for her love life that had been nonexistent since her divorce. Though her past failure in a relationship had made Paula extra cautious and extremely picky, she believed there was still someone out there for her. Just as she was available for the right man. For whatever reason, the new criminology professor at the university, Neil Ramirez, came to mind. Aside from being a drop-dead gorgeous Hispanic, the ATF special agent and renowned criminal profiler seemed to know his stuff in the classroom as a visiting professor, and had proven to be popular among criminology students, from what she understood. Out of curiosity, she had sat in on his lecture a couple of times, only speaking briefly to him afterward, but leaving with a favorable impression nonetheless as someone she could imagine building a rapport with.

She knew little of his backstory, other than that he had recently lost someone close to him, a fellow ATF agent, who was killed in the line of duty. As would be expected, apparently Neil Ramirez took it pretty hard, just as Paula knew would be the case were someone in the department dealt a similar fate. The special agent's reputation as a hardworking, honest and dependable agent made him a valued addition to Addison University and the School of Criminal Justice, both of whom apparently welcomed him with open arms.

Paula was indeed a bit curious about his life off the job. Or if Professor Ramirez even had a life outside of work, which she found herself short on these days. For all she knew, he was happily married and had a few kids to go back to. Paula lamented over never having started a family with her ex and wondered if that might have made a difference in her failed marriage. Or was she grasping at straws for something that had simply run out of steam, no matter how painful it was to have to reconcile herself with that?

She returned to the here and now as she pulled into the parking lot of the Gotley Building on Wakefield Road that housed the Department of Mathematics. After finding a spot, she parked and exited the vehicle. Slender, at five feet nine inches in height, she was wearing a one-button black blazer over a moss-colored satin charmeuse shirt and midrise blue ponte knit pants, along with square-toed flats. Tucked inside her jacket in a leather concealment holster was a SIG Sauer P365 semi-automatic pistol. In a force of habit, she tapped it as if to make sure it was still there, and then ran a hand through her brunette layered and medium-length haircut, parted squarely in the middle, before heading into the building.

On the third floor, where Professor Furillo's office was located, Paula found it already cordoned off by barricade tape, and members of the Crime Scene Investigation Unit were busy at work processing the site. Bypassing them, she was greeted by Detective Mike Davenport.

The tall, forty-year-old married father of three girls was blue-eyed and had short dark locks in a quiff hairstyle and a chevron mustache.

"Hey," he said tonelessly.

"Hey." She gave him a friendly nod and then got down to business. "What's the latest?"

"It's not good." Davenport frowned. "Appears as though Professor Furillo was grading papers when someone took her by surprise," he remarked. "From the looks of it, she apparently fought with her attacker but, unfortunately, came up short. The seat cushion beside the body suggests it was the murder weapon used to suffocate the victim."

Paula wrinkled her dainty nose at him. "And a student discovered her?"

"Yeah. Name's Joan McCashin. Says she had a scheduled meeting with Furillo this morning, came upon the body and then immediately called 911. McCashin's prepared to give a formal statement to that effect."

"Good." Paula glanced over his shoulder. "Which office is the professor's?"

"This one," he answered, leading the way as they passed by two closed office doors to an open door.

Stepping into the small and cramped windowless office, Paula glanced at the gangly and bald-headed crime scene photographer who gave her a nod, then resumed his snapping of pictures routinely, before she spied the deceased associate professor on the floor beside an ergonomic computer desk. Odette Furillo was lying flat on her back on the beige carpeted floor. In her thirties, she was slender and about five-six, blond-haired with brown highlights in a stacked pixie, and fully dressed in a button-front light blue blouse, navy straight-leg pants and black loafers. Next to her head was a gray memory foam office chair pillow. The impressions on it seemed to contour with that of a face when pressed against it.

Cringing, Paula could only imagine the horror of knowing you were about to die and not being able to do a thing to prevent it. Still, she noted what appeared to be blood on one of the hands of the professor, suggesting that she might have scratched her attacker, collecting valuable DNA in the process. "Maybe Professor Furillo got the unsub's DNA to help us ID the killer," Paula pointed out optimistically.

"I was thinking the same thing," Davenport said, knitting his thick brows. "Hopefully the medical examiner and forensics will make that happen and we'll go from there."

"We need to find out who else may have been working in the building last night. That includes students and custodial workers. Let's see what surveillance cameras can tell us." In Paula's way of thinking, no one could be excluded as a suspect, given that more than a few people had access to the Gotley Building.

"Yeah." Davenport scratched his jutting chin. "And then cross-check it with anyone who might have been in the vicinity of the second victim of the alleged Campus Killer on school grounds."

Paula eyed the professor's laptop and wondered if her computer and online activities before, during and after the attack might provide clues about the unsub. "Let's get the Digital Forensics and Cyber Crime Unit over here pronto and see what they can find from the laptop, if anything. Along with Odette Furillo's cell phone," Paula added, noting it on the desktop.

He gave a nod. "Will do."

They heard some chatter and left the office, careful not to taint potential evidence. In the hallway, approaching them was Detective Gayle Yamasaki of the Rendall Cove PD's Detective Bureau. In her midthirties, single and slim with small brown eyes and long, curly black hair tied in a low bun, the pretty Indigenous Hawaiian was heading the investigation into the murder of Professor Debra Newton, who was strangled to death in her apartment in June.

"Came as soon as I got the word," Gayle said, wringing her thin hands. "So, what are we looking at here?"

Paula furrowed her brow. "You can see for yourself, but by all indications, including the appearance of the victim and the killer's MO, we're looking at another homicide courtesy of the Campus Killer."

Gayle sighed and took a peek at the deceased before muttering an expletive. "Four and counting," she groaned.

"Tell me about it." Paula made a face. "We need to find out if the victims were connected in any way." *And if so, how exactly*, she thought.

"Assuming these aren't just random killings," Gayle countered.

"There is that." Paula understood that if they were in fact chasing a single killer, the unsub could just as easily be someone the victims knew as a total stranger. Whatever the case, as they were all professors, that in and of itself indicated some relationship to this institution of higher education.

"The bottom line," Davenport told them, "is that someone is on a killing rampage on this campus and in our town, and it's up to us to stop him."

"There's no other option," Paula agreed, knowing that to think otherwise would be playing right into the unsub's deadly hands. "We have to figure this out, sooner than later."

Shays County Chief Medical Examiner Eddie Saldana arrived, and they parted the way to let him through. In his early fifties, short and of medium build, he had red hair blended with gray in a side-swept style to partially cover his pate and wore square glasses over sharp gray eyes.

"This is getting to be a bad habit," he grumbled, frowning.

"One we're all hoping to kick," Paula said humorlessly. "Whatever you can give us on the deceased would be helpful in that regard, Dr. Saldana."

"I'll see what I can do." He stepped into Odette Furillo's office and, after squeezing into nitrile gloves, methodically did a quick examination of the victim, before saying glumly, "All things considered, my initial assessment is that the professor likely died as a result of violent asphyxia. I'll be more definitive once the autopsy is completed, including an estimation of the time of death."

Even the preliminary conclusion was more than enough to convince Paula that this was not only a homicide, but one that mirrored the three other deaths attributed to a single killer with a singular modus operandi. "We'll look forward to reading the autopsy report when it's ready," she told him, which Paula assumed would be the next day. Until then, they needed to do whatever was necessary to try to gather evidence and build a case toward eventually pinning the crime on the one responsible.

THE CAMPUS KILLER relished this opportunity to catch the action, hidden very much in plain view. Endless chatter about the death of Professor Odette Furillo seemed to grip those around him, as though it was the worst possible thing that could happen. Actually, even worse for those standing around would be if they themselves suffered the same fate as the attractive Honors College associate professor. He laughed inside. As it was, they were not the targets of his murderous ways. Unfortunately, the same could not be said of the other three pretty professors who managed to find their way into his crosshairs and were given a one-way ticket to an early death.

He mused about the campus and city police trying to stop him in his deadly tracks. They were undoubtedly freaking out about his uncanny ability to run rings around them while handpicking his victims right under the authorities' collective noses. Another laugh rang in his head as he wound his way through the bystanders, speaking only when spoken to. And even then, limiting what he said and how he said it, so as not to tip his hand in the slightest as to his guilt. For all they could see, he was merely one of them, content with complaining and speculating about the homicides, but otherwise keeping the worst of it at a safe distance so as not to be contaminated like spoiled food.

He watched as the good-looking female university detective left the building, seemingly in a huff, while giving only a cursory glance his way, as one of many. Not having the slightest clue that she was looking at the

Campus Killer and was within her power to take him
into custody. Except that she never really saw him for
who he was. Just as he anticipated when making himself visible as part of the thrill from the kill.

As Detective Paula Lynley headed down the sidewalk, he resisted the desire to follow her, deciding it
was more of a risk than he was willing to take at this
time. Something, though, told him that an opportunity
would likely present itself for them to meet face-to-face.
At which time, she would very likely regret having ever
laid eyes on him in ways she would never see coming.

Till it was much too late.

OUTSIDE THE BUILDING, some professors and students
milled about aimlessly, probably in somewhat of a state
of shock, while likely wondering when and if they would
be let back inside. Or perhaps, Paula considered, if and
when it would be safe to do so. She wondered the same
thing herself. Or, for that matter, when the entire campus could go back to normal, without the looming threat
of a serial killer hanging in the air like an unsettling
dark rain cloud.

Short of solving this case overnight, Paula suspected
that her boss would soon be sending out a request to the
FBI to join in on the investigation. A routine thing when
it came to creating serial killer task forces and utilizing
the far reach of federal law enforcement and seemingly
unlimited resources of the federal government. She had
seen this all too often when married to an FBI agent,
who also had a brother working in the Bureau. At the
very least, Paula believed that a behavioral profiler was

needed to help them better size up who and what they were after in the dangerous and lethal unsub.

This brought Neil Ramirez back to the forefront of her thoughts. As a criminal profiler, who also happened to be an expert on violent serial offenders from what she learned during one of his lectures, the professor was just the person they needed to utilize his expertise in their current investigation. Would he be up to the task? Or would his professional demons stand in the way? Those notwithstanding, she was sure that Captain McNamara would welcome Neil Ramirez into the fold as a paid consultant. As would Gayle Yamasaki and her boss with the Rendall Cove PD's Detective Bureau, Criminal Investigations Sergeant Anderson Klimack.

Paula walked to Horton Hall, three buildings over on Creighten Road, where Professor Ramirez was currently giving a lecture. She was eager to speak with him and a bit nervous at the same time, though unsure if that was due to her impending request. Or the sheer presence of the good-looking man himself.

The latter was on full display as she slipped in the back of the packed room, but had no trouble sizing up the ATF special agent, filling in the blanks of her memory. Standing in front of the class, Neil Ramirez was a good six feet, three inches tall at least, and rock solid in a way that could only come from regular workouts and a healthy diet. His thick brown hair was cut in a high razor fade. He had a diamond-shaped, square-jawed face, gray-brown eyes that shone in their intensity, and sported a heavy stubble beard that looked really good on him. Wearing a red Henley shirt, black jeans and tennis shoes, he seemed to fit right in as a college professor.

When he seemed to home in on her, Paula's heart did a little leap and check. But just as quickly, as if she had suddenly become invisible to him, Professor Ramirez turned in a different direction as he talked about profiling a criminal, giving Paula time to catch her breath and put together enough of a sell to bring him on board.

VISITING CRIMINOLOGY PROFESSOR NEIL RAMIREZ would've had to be foolish not to notice the stunning African American detective sergeant with the Department of Police and Public Safety at the college, Paula Lynley. As it was, his sight was better than twenty-twenty the last time he had his eyes examined, and he had no trouble seeing what was staring him right in the face, more or less. In fact, he'd been checking her out each time she decided to pay his lecture a visit. And even once or twice when he happened to notice her elsewhere on campus from afar. Tall and well put together on a slim frame, she thoroughly captivated the detective with her caramel complexion, heart-shaped face, big and pretty brown eyes, delicate nose, wide mouth and most generous smile. She had a stylish look to the chestnut brown hair grazing her shoulders.

Though they had exchanged a few words now and then, Neil had resisted going beyond the surface in getting to know the detective better. Still dealing with some personal and professional issues, he had chosen for the time being to focus on just trying to fit in to his temporary new world of teaching college students about criminology, criminal justice and criminal profiling.

As a thirty-six-year-old Mexican American special agent with the Bureau of Alcohol, Tobacco, Firearms and Explosives, Neil had gone through the ATF National Academy, located at the Federal Law Enforcement Training Center in Glynco, Georgia, and been assigned to the Federal Bureau of Investigation's Behavioral Analysis Unit to earn his stripes. Before that, he had graduated from the University of Arizona in Tucson with a Bachelor of Science in Criminal Justice Studies and a focus on Social and Behavioral Sciences. Now, thirteen years into his career, he was primarily working out of the ATF's field office in Grand Rapids, Michigan, as a behavioral profiler and providing technical support in ATF, FBI or task force investigations.

Neil lamented as he pondered the death of his colleague, Ramone Munoz, who died during a shoot-out last year with drug traffickers as a member of the ATF Special Response Team. Between that and Neil's breakup with his girlfriend, Constance Chen, who went looking for another man and found him in a musician, Neil had decided to take a step back from his full-time duties as a special agent, giving him some time to clear his head.

With a bestselling book on criminal profiling to his credit, he accepted a position as a visiting professor with Addison University's School of Criminal Justice this past summer. The short-term contract left the door open for a longer commitment both ways, if all went well. But Neil wasn't looking beyond the current fall semester at this point. Especially since he had also been tasked by the ATF with gathering intel on a suspected arms trafficking operation in Rendall Cove that had been uncovered through chatter on the dark web. With an undercover agent on the inside working with the Rendall Cove Police Department's Firearms Investigation Unit and the

Shays County Sheriff's Department, Neil was confident they would be successful in putting the brakes on this purported online trafficking in contraband firearms and ammunition operation, as well as unlawful possession of arms and ammunition.

Neil forced himself to take his eyes off the detective just long enough to snap out of the trance. He gazed at Paula Lynley again, curious as to why she was there. *Maybe she'll decide to fill me in,* he thought. It wasn't lost on him that an investigation was underway between the school's DPPS and the city's police department involving the murders of three female professors. Were they actually connected? Was there a single perp involved? It admittedly piqued the interest of the profiler in him. Up to a point.

He turned back to his students, remembering how difficult it was when he was in college to hold his attention. So far, so good. They seemed to be buying what he was selling in offering them a well-rounded look at criminality and the devious minds of hard-core criminals. But for how long?

When the class ended, Neil finished routinely with, "We'll pick it up the next time. But don't let that stop you from heading over to the library, where I've got some books on reserve, for further insight into the subject matter."

After the students, about half male and half female, began filing out of the classroom, Neil watched Paula Lynley come forward in measured steps as he was placing some papers into his faux-leather briefcase. He grinned at her and said curiously, "Detective Lynley. Nice to see you again." He met her eyes for a long moment, trying to read into them but having little luck. "So, what brings you to my class this morning?"

She held his gaze and, without preface, responded straightforwardly, "Professor Ramirez, I need your help."

Chapter Two

Paula was momentarily at a loss for follow-up words as she took in the very good-looking visiting professor. It somehow seemed easier to approach him when it was just a hello in passing than when she had to seek his assistance in an important criminal investigation. But rather than chicken out like a schoolgirl with a crush on the star quarterback, she managed to gather herself and say coolly, "I'm sure you're aware that three female professors at the university have been murdered over the past three months."

Neil nodded to that effect. "Yeah, I know about it," he said cautiously. "Sad thing."

"That's putting it mildly." Paula took a breath. "This morning, a fourth professor was found murdered in her office."

"What?" He cocked a slightly crooked brow. "I hadn't heard about that one," he confessed.

"We're just getting the word out, while trying to wrap our minds around the fact that this is happening at all."

"Has anyone been arrested?" Neil seemed to rethink the question. "I assume that would be a no?"

"Correct assumption." She lifted her chin. "Unfortunately, the unsub is still on the loose and obviously has to be considered as possibly armed and definitely dangerous," she pointed out. "But as of now, we don't believe there is an immediate threat to students and staff, per se. That could change, of course, as more info comes in on the homicide."

He regarded her with interest, then asked with a catch in his voice, "So, what exactly did you need from me?"

Paula pushed a strand of hair away from her forehead and responded frankly, "Your expertise as a profiler, Professor Ramirez. Or should I say Special Agent Ramirez?"

"Neil will be fine, Detective Lynley," he told her evenly.

"Okay, Neil. And please call me Paula," she said, feeling as though they had already broken the ice in getting what she needed from him. "Anyway, it appears as if we're dealing with a serial killer here that the press has already dubbed the Campus Killer. The Department of Police and Public Safety is working with the Rendall Cove PD to bring the perp to justice and solve the case. In the meantime, we can use all the help we can get in developing a profile on the unsub to aid in the investigation. As a visiting professor who also happens to be a criminal profiler, I thought I'd reach out to see if you'd be interested in working with us as a paid consultant on the case?"

Neil rubbed his prominent jawline. "I kind of have my hands full at the moment," he said ambivalently. "Teaching these kids can be exhausting."

Though in complete agreement from her own college years and dealing with some of the misbehaving students today, Paula locked eyes with him and responded sharply, "So can murder. I understand that you're here to teach.

But keeping them safe is even more important, don't you think? I could reach out to the FBI, as long as it isn't to my ex-husband," she found herself saying candidly. "However, since you're on campus, I wanted to give it a go first." She realized she was putting him on the spot unfairly, but desperation at times called for dirty tactics.

Neil gave her an amused grin. "Since you put it that way, ex-husband and all, I'll be happy to come aboard as a profiler in your investigation."

"Thanks." Paula blushed. "I'm sure that tapping into your expertise will give us some valuable insight into the unsub, before and after apprehension."

"Why don't you email me what you have on the unsub and case," Neil said, "and I'll take a look for a preliminary assessment."

"I'll do that," she promised, excited at the prospect of getting to know him. At least on a professional basis.

He nodded and grabbed his briefcase. "I'll walk you out."

Paula smiled, leading the way into the hall. "So, how's it been teaching, compared to working out in the field as an ATF agent?" She immediately saw the question as too trivial.

Neil laughed. "Well, for one, the teaching is mostly inside and investigations for the ATF are often outside. But apart from that difference, I have to say, I love trying to influence young minds, even if only for a short while, whereas I'm not as keen on having to take down the bad guys these days. But that's a story for another time..." He frowned thoughtfully. "Anyway, it's a good living, so I suppose I shouldn't complain."

Paula considered the tragedy he'd experienced with

the death of a fellow agent. She wondered if there was more that soured him on working for the ATF. Maybe there would be another time to get the scoop. "Believe me," she told him, "we all have professional complaints from time to time. Comes with the territory." Not that she had issues with her current employer, but she knew that there were always good and bad days for every job. Hers was no exception. Such as now, when she was dealing with a serial perp and needed it solved sooner than later.

"You're right, of course," he said. "Life is always about what you make of it, for better or worse."

"True." Neil brushed shoulders with her and Paula immediately felt an electrical spark surge through her. Had he experienced this as well? At the door to the outside, he flashed a sideways grin and said, "My office is on the third floor."

She smiled, understanding that he was headed there and, as such, this was where they parted. "Thanks for agreeing to work with us," she expressed.

"I'm happy to do what I can to help out." He opened the door for her and said, "By the way, no pay is necessary to consult on the case as a profiler. Consider it an extension of my work as a visiting professor that maybe my students can learn a thing or two from."

"If you say so." Paula welcomed his involvement, whatever the terms. And she did believe that his criminal justice students stood to benefit from whatever he chose to bring to the table. As she would herself, she believed.

Out of Horton Hall, Paula headed for her car, equipped with a new weapon in the ongoing investigation.

Neil Ramirez.

NEIL WATCHED FOR a moment as Paula Lynley walked away from the building. He found himself undressing her in his mind, sure he would like every bit of what he saw. How could he not? Coming back down to earth, he knew that he needed to stay on another track where it concerned the police detective sergeant. At least till he had a chance to get a read on the so-called Campus Killer. Then maybe the vibes he'd picked up when they touched shoulders—or even met each other's eyes—might be something to explore further. Or was the sour taste in his mouth from his last failed relationship still bitter enough not to want to jump back in the ring with another woman?

Inside his temporary office, Neil sat at the L-shaped computer desk in a well-worn brown faux-leather chair and mused about the lovely detective he would be working with. So, she'd been married to an FBI agent. Any children in the marriage before they parted ways? How did Paula's ex ever let her get away? Or was it a mutual thing of simply growing apart and wanting something different in their lives?

Neil wondered if she was seeing anyone right now. Or was Paula cautious about opening her heart to another man any time soon? If so, could he really blame her? Was he any less guilty of preferring not to rush into anything these days? Then again, would it be foolish not to keep an open mind for the right person, whenever she entered his orbit?

His thoughts moved back to the consulting as a profiler job he'd just agreed to. He questioned just how advisable it was to take on another assignment with his plate already full. Since when had that ever stopped him? He always tried to do what was best in any given situation. In this instance, how could he not agree to assist in the case, with what sure looked like a serial killer lurking on and around the campus? One who threatened the lives of female professors. And could easily target female students as well, if the unsub was not stopped.

Paula drew a hard bargain, Neil told himself, sitting back. He looked forward to reviewing the particulars of the case and lending his knowledge in the hunt for the killer. Beyond that, Neil still had to deal with the fact that a suspected arms trafficker was also in their midst and needed to be brought under control before unleashing more gun violence in Rendall Cove and abroad.

PAULA PARKED IN the employee parking lot of the Addison University Police Department on Cedar Lane. She went inside the building and headed straight for the office of Captain Shailene McNamara. After being waved in, Paula stepped through the door. Shailene was at her standing desk on the phone. She studied the captain, who was fifty years old, on the slender side and had strawberry blond hair styled in a choppy bob. Her blues eyes looked bigger behind prescription eyeglasses. Shailene was on her second marriage and the mother of four children.

She ended the call and, gazing at Paula, said, "So, where are we on the case?"

Reiterating what had already been reported, Paula filled her in with more details on Associate Professor Odette Furillo's murder, which fell short of naming a suspect. Or having the official cause of her death, pending release of the autopsy report. Then, as Paula watched the captain's expression meander between frustration and resignation, she told her, "I've asked Visiting Professor Neil Ramirez to join the investigation as a criminal profiler."

Shailene perked up upon hearing this. "Really?"

"Yes. Given his expertise on killers, including serial killers, it seemed like a good idea to take advantage of the ATF special agent's presence at Addison University. To pick his brain, if you will," Paula stressed.

"A very good idea." Shailene nodded in agreement. "With the murder of four of our professors, at this point, getting Agent Ramirez on board is a smart move." She touched her glasses. "I take it he accepted the offer?"

"Yes," Paula was happy to announce. "Moreover, Neil doesn't want any compensation, believing that it's his duty as a visiting professor and profiler to lend a hand to the investigation."

Shailene's face lit with approval. "Actually, I read Agent Ramirez's book on profiling. Good stuff. You should check it out, when you get a chance."

"I will." Paula exchanged a few more thoughts while glancing about the spacious office with its contemporary furnishings and plaques on the wall. When Shailene's cell phone rang, it was Paula's excuse to leave.

En route to her own office, she ran into Detective Mike Davenport. "Hey," she said to him.

"Hey." His broad shoulders squared. "Got some info for you."

"Okay." She met his eyes with curiosity. "Why don't we step into my office?"

"All right."

He followed her into the corner office, which Davenport had once thought would be his, until Paula got it instead, after being promoted to detective sergeant.

Though things had been a little tense between them for a while, he had seemingly gotten past the disappointment and they were in a good place right now, as far as Paula was concerned. She believed Davenport was a good detective and valued having him on her squad.

Rather than essentially pulling rank by taking a seat at her three-drawer desk and inviting him to sit on one of the two vinyl black stacking chairs on the other side, Paula remained standing. Eyeing the detective, she asked, "So, what do you have?"

Davenport ran a hand through his hair and replied matter-of-factly, "Well, I was able to pull up security camera footage from inside and outside the Gotley Building, where Professor Odette Furillo was killed. Seems as though a number of people, mostly students by the look of it, were out and about, along with vehicles, between last night and this morning. Once we get the official time of death, we can better sort through them and see if we can narrow down potential suspects."

"Good." Paula nodded, expecting to get this information from the autopsy report in the morning. "Anything else?"

"Yeah," he said. "As expected, we'll be checking out any cell phones that pinged around the time Furillo was murdered. And, of course, we're waiting to see if there's DNA to work with in unmasking the unsub."

Paula smiled thinly, knowing they were going about this the right way. "I have some news too," she told him.

"What's that?"

She told him about Neil Ramirez agreeing to work with them. "As a criminal profiler, Professor Ramirez should give us some crucial insight into the killer," she finished.

"I agree." Davenport bobbed his head. "Heard about Ramirez's successes in helping to nab some perps. If he's willing to step away from teaching long enough to profile our unsub, more power to him. It's all about solving the case and making the campus and surroundings a safe environment again, right?"

"Absolutely." Paula showed her teeth, glad to see that he didn't believe Neil was somehow using his fed credentials as an ATF special agent to take over the case. On the contrary, she believed that the visiting professor was an asset, lending his skills in teaming up with the DPPS's Investigative Division and the Rendall Cove PD's Detective Bureau in their pursuit of justice.

After Davenport left the office, Paula sat in her ergonomic mid-back leather desk chair and phoned Gayle Yamasaki to let her know that Neil Ramirez would be assisting them.

"That's wonderful," Gayle expressed. "Seems that Agent Ramirez's reputation as a profiler precedes him."

Paula chuckled. "Appears that way."

"What have you gotten out of him so far?"

"Not much. I'm sending him the info we have on the unsub shortly."

"Can't wait to get his take on the perp," Gayle said.

"Same here," Paula had to admit, as if Neil's assessment alone could nab the unsub. If only it were that simple. As it was, cracking this case had been anything but simple, thus far. Only diligence in their collective efforts would lead to favorable results.

Later, Paula copied some digital files, emailed them

to Neil and did some paperwork. Her thoughts drifted here and there between her former married life and the present, where she was divorced but still wanting to be in a stable relationship with respect that was mutual and not one-sided. She couldn't help but wonder if this was something that Neil was looking for too in a partner. Had he left someone behind during his current stint on campus? Or was he seeing someone locally these days?

Better not allow my imagination to run wild, Paula scolded herself, no matter how tempting to do so.

After work, she headed over to the campus bookstore on Blaire Street and picked up a copy of Neil's book, entitled appropriately, *Profiling the Killers*. From there, Paula stopped off at Burger King and ordered a fish sandwich and onion rings for takeout, not in the mood for making dinner.

She drove home, which was an upscale penthouse condominium in Northwest Rendall Cove on Sadler Lane, a block from Rendall Creek Park. Exiting her car in covered parking, Paula bypassed the elevator and scaled the flights of stairs to her two-bedroom, two-bath fourth-story unit. The two-level unit had an open concept, with a nice great room and engineered eucalyptus hardwood flooring. Floor-to-ceiling windows and a covered deck overlooked a creek, where Canada geese loved to hang out, and pawpaw trees. She had picked out some great rustic furnishings and accent pieces for downstairs. The gourmet kitchen came with granite countertops and stainless steel appliances.

Sitting in a corner of the kitchen, as though waiting for Paula to come home, was her cat. She'd had the female Devon rex for a year now, named it Chloe, and thought she was adorable. Setting her Burger King bag on the counter, Paula scooped up the medium-sized cat and said, "Bet you're hungry too, huh?"

Chloe purred lovingly. Paula set her down on the floor, put some shredded chicken cat food in a bowl and watched as Chloe went for it hungrily. After heading up the quarter-turn staircase to the second floor, Paula stepped into the spacious bedroom with its large windows and farmhouse-style furniture, where she removed her sidearm and holster, before freshening up in the en suite.

Back downstairs, she poured herself a glass of white wine and ate her meal standing up, while watching Chloe scamper off as if having something better to do than hang out with her, now that she had been fed. Paula finished eating and took the wineglass with her to the great room, where she sat on a barrel club chair and started to read Neil's book with interest.

NEIL HAD RENTED the custom and newly built, two-story home in a subdivision on Leary Way in Rendall Cove at the start of the summer session. It was right across the street from Rendall Creek Park. He still maintained his colonial-style house on a few acres of land in Grand Rapids. But for the time being, he was living in this college town and making the most of his surroundings, which included a woodland behind the house with a running trail. Inside, it had crown molding and a symmetrical layout with wide open spaces and interesting angles, a high ceiling, large windows, vinyl plank flooring, a traditional kitchen with an island and an informal dining room. It came fully furnished with modern chairs and tables.

Basically, the place had everything he needed and more, Neil believed. If he didn't count living there alone when, deep down inside, he would have preferred sharing his space with someone who actually wanted to be there. Maybe that day would come again. Or maybe he was asking for too much, after what turned out to be a debacle in his last relationship.

With a bottle of beer in hand, Neil sat on a solid wood leisure chair in the living room and opened up his laptop. He accessed the files Paula had sent him on the Campus Killer case. Since June, there had been one, two, three and now four murders to occur on and off the college grounds, with all the victims female professors. Each victim had been suffocated by the unsub, who somehow managed to get away, with little to tie the perp to the murders.

"Hmm," Neil muttered out loud. He was sensing a distinct pattern among the homicides. One that was hard to ignore for a profiler. The actions by what appeared to be a serial killer were deliberate and methodical. In Neil's mind, the perp—most likely a male by serial murder standards—had to have been stalking the victims, targeting them one by one.

Tasting the beer, Neil took a sharp breath, knowing that the unsub would almost certainly not call it quits. Being successful in the killings thus far was only inviting the perpetrator to strike again when the opportunity presented itself.

That thought was perhaps scariest of all.

Chapter Three

The following afternoon, the Campus Killer Task Force assembled in a Department of Police and Public Safety conference room at the university for the latest information on the investigation. Paula, who got little sleep last night after reading Neil Ramirez's entire book on profiling, was happy that he showed up today with her invitation. She was mindful that even with his participation in the case, he still had his duties as a visiting professor that had to be respected.

As much as I might like to, I can't hog up all of the special agent's time, Paula thought, as she gave him a friendly nod before she took to the podium. She glanced at Mike Davenport and Gayle Yamasaki, both of whom would have something to say in the scheme of things, and then Paula got down to business. Grabbing a stylus pen, she turned to the large touch-screen monitor and brought up an image of the first victim.

"In June, Debra Newton, a thirty-three-year-old associate professor in the School of Journalism, was smothered to death in her apartment on Frandor Lane in Rendall Cove." Paula was glad that, for the purpose of identifying them today, they had photos of the victims when they were alive and healthy, rather than their melancholy images after death. She regarded the attractive, white, blue-eyed professor with long wavy crimson locks and feathered bangs. "Professor Newton was divorced and had no known enemies, but obviously ended up with a real target on her back."

Paula switched to another image of a striking Latina, with pretty brown eyes and long, straight brunette hair, and said, "In July, thirty-four-year-old Harmeet Fernández, an assistant professor in the Department of Horticulture, was found dead in the Horticulture Gardens on Moxlyn Place, due to suffocation. She had just broken off what was described as a contentious relationship with a fellow professor, Clayton Ricamara. His alibi of being at an economics conference in London when she was killed held up."

After taking a breath, Paula brought up on the screen a picture of an attractive African American woman with blondish boho braids and big sable eyes, before saying, "In August, Kathy Payne, a thirty-six-year-old professor in the College of Veterinary Medicine, was murdered in the same fashion in her Rendall Cove residence on Belle Street. Dr. Payne was a widow and not known to be seeing anyone at the time of her death."

The last image Paula put on the monitor was of a gorgeous white woman with long blond hair with brown highlights in a stacked pixie and green eyes. "In September, just yesterday morning, Odette Furillo, a thirty-four-year-old recently separated associate professor in the Department of Mathematics, was discovered on the floor of her office in the Gotley Building on Wakefield Road. According to the autopsy report from the county chief medical examiner, Professor Furillo's death was ruled a homicide, with the cause being asphyxia. Estimated time of death was somewhere between eight p.m. and eleven p.m."

Paula sighed and furrowed her brow. "All four homicide victims were suffocated to death by whom we believe to be the same unknown assailant. There is no evidence that any of the women were victims of a sexual assault. While we are still gathering and processing information, as of now, this unsub remains at large and can be considered extremely dangerous for female professors specifically, and all women who spend time on campus or who reside in the local community—so long as the perp is able to dodge being identified and taken into custody." Paula gazed at Neil, who seemed attentive in gazing back at her. "To that end, we've brought on board ATF Special Agent and criminal profiler, Neil Ramirez, who's currently doing double duty as a visiting professor of criminal justice. Agent Ramirez will give us his take on our unsub. But first, Detectives Mike Davenport and Gayle Yamasaki will provide updates on the investigation."

Paula gave both a brief smile and waited for them to come up and take her place. Davenport put a friendly hand on her shoulder and said in earnest, "This isn't easy for any of us, but we'll get through it and solve the case, one way or the other."

Paula nodded. "I know," she agreed, while feeling that day couldn't come soon enough for all concerned.

Gayle said to her, "You nailed it in setting things up, Paula, especially for our newcomer, Neil Ramirez. Hope I can add a bit more clarity on my end of the investigation."

"I'm sure you will," she told her with confidence, as

Paula squeezed her hand and walked off to the side. She glanced at Neil, eager to hear what he had to say, especially after reading his excellent book last night.

Gayle went through the backstories on Debra Newton and Kathy Payne, the two professors killed off campus. Gayle was operating as the lead investigator with the Rendall Cove PD in trying to piece together some of the similarities in the homicides beyond the surface, which included relatively easy points of entry into the residences and lack of security systems. In an annoyed tone of voice, she concluded, "It's pretty clear that our unsub is deliberately choosing to rotate the kills off and on campus, perhaps to throw us off the trail, or otherwise play a deadly game of cat and mouse. We have to find a way to turn the tables and stop this before it gets much worse for both our police departments."

She stepped away from the podium and Davenport took her place. He wasted little time in getting to the heart of the evidence in the latest murder at Addison University, as Davenport said evenly, "As you all know, we have surveillance cameras covering most locations on campus. Kind of makes it tough to do something bad and slip away quietly, even in the dark of night. At least not so we can't eventually track you down. I've had a chance to take a look at video recorded on campus the night that Professor Odette Furillo was murdered."

Lifting the stylus pen, he brought security camera footage to the large screen. "What you see is surveillance video taken outside the Gotley Building, where Furillo's office is located, around the estimated time of her death. Here, on the south side of the building, you can see what appears to be a white man moving away quickly on foot, as if he'd just seen a ghost. But more likely, it was because he had just committed a heinous crime and was making his getaway."

Paula homed in on the monitor. Though the video was grainy, it was clear enough to see that the unsub did seem to be an adult male who was tall, solid in build and wearing dark clothing and a hoodie, obviously intended as a deliberate means to camouflage his appearance. He was certainly making haste in vacating the building and surroundings. Was this their Campus Killer?

The man's making a good case for being guilty of something, Paula told herself.

"We're still studying other surveillance camera video, with different angles and distance from the Gotley Building, to see if the unsub got into a vehicle and where else he might have gone," Davenport pointed out. "As well as to see if any other serious suspects might emerge, given the timeline. But as of now, I'd have to say that the man you see is definitely a person of interest we need to track down."

Paula couldn't agree more, and she glanced at Neil to see him nod his head in concurrence. She turned back to Davenport, who was saying, "DNA was collected from beneath the fingernails of Furillo. As this doesn't belong to the professor, the forensic unknown profile was sent to CODIS, in hopes of getting a hit in the database of convicted offender or arrestee DNA profiles, or forensic indexes from crime scenes." He frowned. "Unfortunately, there was no match. Looks like the unsub isn't in the system. But we have this DNA sample and we have a person of interest on our radar. We just need to find him, interrogate him, compare his DNA with the unidentified DNA profile and see what happens."

With any luck, we'll be able to do just that, Paula mused, optimistic that they could and would track down the suspect.

When Davenport was through, she reintroduced Neil to those in attendance as he stood and approached her.

NEIL TOOK IN everything that was said as he shook the hands of Paula, noting how soft her skin was, Gayle Yamasaki and lastly Mike Davenport, who said to him, "Great to have you as part of the team, Agent Ramirez."

"Thanks." Neil noted that he had a firm grip in the handshake, matching his own. "Happy to help in any way I can." As the detectives walked away, he regarded the members of the task force, having already been acquainted with some from the Rendall Cove PD, doing double duty, like him, with the Firearms Investigation Unit. "First, let me say thanks to everyone here for bringing me up to speed on what I didn't know when looking at it from a small distance as a visiting professor. Hopefully, the surveillance video and DNA evidence will lead to an arrest soon. As a criminal profiler and ATF special agent, I doubt that it would surprise many of you in my belief that, based on the modus operandi in the murders, it's a safe bet that we are looking at a serial killer in our midst." In his mind, Neil considered that these days the FBI defined even two such homicides fitting the criteria as serial murders. Double that number and it left little doubt that they were dealing with a serial killer.

"On the other hand, you may or may not know that serial killers operating on university campuses and in college towns is far from unusual," Neil had to say. "Quite the contrary, with the warm and fuzzy welcoming environment and relatively easy and multiple escape routes. In many ways, this is the perfect setting for serial killers to prey upon victims. Think of Ted Bundy, John Norman Collins and Donald Miller, to name a few, all of whom went after female college students—any of which among the predators could just as easily have turned their deadly attention to female professors."

Neil allowed that to sink in for a moment and then continued, "As for this so-called Campus Killer, my early read is that the unsub is obviously someone who has knowledge of the campus and its surroundings— such as a professor, student or university employee— and uses it to his advantage to target those whom he has likely stalked surreptitiously and gone after when most advantageous to him. I see the unsub as a narcissistic, opportunistic vulture, who likely has a giant chip on his shoulder and has chosen to use this to go after the women whom he may deem as beneath him or think they are better than him. He could have been rejected by one or more of the victims," Neil reasoned. "Or simply used rejection of his advances or desires in general to target these victims who, through one means or another, came into his crosshairs."

Davenport, who was standing off to the side, asked him curiously, "What are your thoughts on the racial and ethnic mixture of the victims? Is this the unsub's way of saying he hates all women? Or at least those who are involved in higher education as educators?"

"Good question," Neil acknowledged. As it was, the differences between the four victims in terms of being white, African American and Hispanic were not lost on him. He contemplated this for a moment or two, then responded coolly, "I don't see this as hating all women, per se. Or racist. Or even the unsub fancying himself as an equal opportunity serial killer. More likely, it's a ruse or smoke screen, meant more to throw the investigation off by questioning the nature of the attacks, rather than the real reason behind them. My guess is that the perp may have homed in on one victim, in particular— whether acquainted with or a complete stranger, and not necessarily the first—then cleverly mixed up the other murders, by race or ethnicity, to make it more difficult to identify the culprit and bring him to justice."

"So, Agent Ramirez, is there any chance the unsub will save us the trouble of capturing him by turning himself in, with the guilt eating away at him like an insidious cancer inside his body?" Gayle threw out seriously.

"Afraid there's little chance of that," he responded honestly. "In my experience of profiling serial killers, in particular, and observations of the lot, in general, very few have a case of conscience where it concerns owning up to what they have done. Certainly not where it concerns walking into a police station and giving up. Unfortunately, most such killers have no wish to be captured and held accountable for their crimes. And few will actually stop killing, as long as the fever for continuing to victimize persists and the risk for detection remains low, in their minds."

"Figured as much." She made a face. "Had to ask."

"Of course." Neil flashed a small smile. "That's why we're here."

Paula, who had taken a seat, leaned forward and asked

directly, "What else can you tell us about the unsub's psyche that might be helpful in understanding who we're up against, in terms of what to look for in our pursuit? As well as when we have him in custody…or have eliminated the threat."

Neil knew that in that last point, she was referring to the reality that the unsub might choose not to surrender when given the opportunity, leaving them no choice but to take him out. As far as he was concerned, Neil preferred that the Campus Killer, if convicted, spent the rest of his life behind bars. But that would be up to him, by and large. Gazing at Paula, Neil responded to her question. "With respect to the psyche of the killer, we're definitely talking about ASPD here—antisocial personality disorder," he stressed, lifting his shoulders. "The unsub's not delusional, based on his actions and skillful ability to have avoided capture thus far. But his penchant for such antisocial behavior with little regard for the human lives he's taking makes him a serious threat to the public, for as long as he's on the loose. I see the unsub as both control-driven and hedonistic in his killings," Neil told her. "That is to say, he gets off on having the power to decide when they live and die."

Paula wrinkled her nose. "What a creep."

"And some other choice words might apply too," Neil said thoughtfully.

"How about the off campus, then on it again killing pattern of the unsub?" she wondered. "Is there some method to this? Or is he merely toying with us in this regard?"

Taking a moment to consider what was an inevitable question, Neil answered evenly, "My guess is that it's largely an attempt by the unsub to keep us guessing by targeting professors on campus and off. But he could also be more haphazard and opportunistic in his MO, whereby he picks his prey and location to murder based upon whatever he deems the most effective and least vulnerable to himself for exposure."

"Hmm…" Paula smoothed an eyebrow. "What about some of the other dynamics, like character traits and background of the unsub, that may be a factor in his homicidal behavior?"

"In this regard, the unsub is just as likely to have come from a stable family as to have been a victim of child abuse and/or broken home," Neil made clear. "And be in a current relationship as much as a loner, and vice versa. He probably supplements his murderous appetite by using alcohol, illegal drugs or both, as an added means to drive him to kill. Whether or not the unsub has been motivated by other serial killers who have made news over the years, such as Bundy, Jeffrey Dahmer, John Wayne Gacy or even Jack the Ripper—or, for that matter, the plethora of true crime documentaries on cable and streaming television or the internet—could go either way."

"Got it," Paula told him, with an amused catch to her voice.

She offered him a weak smile to imply TMI, but Neil took it as more of an indication of satisfaction that he had laid out a solid foundation about the unsub to work with. He suspected that she may have wanted him to go even further in profiling the perpetrator. He was happy to oblige, but didn't want to overdo it by getting too academic or technical in advancing his remarks, at the risk of losing his audience and, in the process, any usefulness in applying this to the investigation.

If the case went on much longer, Neil could see himself adjusting his characterization of the unsub accordingly. But for now, he needed to see how this played out and hope they could get the bead on the Campus Killer sooner than later.

AFTER THE TASK force meeting ended, Paula approached Neil, who was chatting with Davenport, and invited them both to join her and some others for a drink at Blanes Tavern, a local hangout for cops. It had been Gayle who prodded her to ask him. Not that she needed much prodding concerning Neil, as Paula welcomed being able to spend more time with him. Between reading his book and listening to his characterization of the Campus Killer unsub, she was even more fascinated with the man, professionally and personally.

Davenport responded first, saying, "Wish I could. Unfortunately, I have to get home to the missus, who keeps me on a short leash, and my girls, adorable as they are."

"I understand." Paula smiled, envious of him as a family man. She turned her attention to Neil, wondering if this was a path he too was interested in going down, if given the chance. "What about you?"

His jaw clenched as Neil responded musingly, "Sorry, I'll have to pass too. Already have plans."

"I see. No problem," she assured him, even while wondering just what those plans might be. Perhaps to get together with someone he was dating? Would it be so surprising that he had a love life, even if she didn't at the moment?

"Rain check?" he threw out, as if a lifeline.

"Yes, that works for me," she told him, not wanting to put either of them on the spot for making any plans beyond that.

"Great." He favored her with a sideways grin.

Paula smiled back and walked away from the two men, while wondering if they were comparing notes on the investigation. Or her.

"Will they be joining us?" Gayle asked, approaching her.

"Afraid not," Paula almost hated to say. "Both have other things on their plates this evening."

"Too bad." Gayle frowned. "Oh, well. I think we can survive with whomever shows up."

"Agreed." Paula glanced over her shoulder and caught Neil spying on her, alone, as Davenport had already left the room. This eye contact seemed to be the trigger for Neil to follow suit, while avoiding her.

Campus Killer

Chapter Four

Damn, Neil muttered to himself as he left the Department of Police and Public Safety. He regretted missing out on the opportunity to hang with Paula in a more relaxed setting than a task force meeting. Or even a classroom, for that matter. He expected other opportunities would present themselves, as he definitely wanted the chance to get to know the detective sergeant better.

Unfortunately, in this instance, duty called. He had a prescheduled meeting with the ATF undercover surveillance agent, Vinny Ortiz, working on the inside in their arms trafficking investigation. Neil couldn't afford to jeopardize the mission, even if Paula Lynley had managed to occupy a portion of his thoughts.

He climbed into his dark gray Chevrolet Suburban High Country and texted Ortiz to say he would be there in ten minutes. Neil drove off while running through his mind the ultimate goal of getting illegal weapons off the streets, both at home and in other countries when coming from the United States.

Turning onto Prairie Street, his thoughts switched to the Campus Killer investigation. The task force seemed well suited to solve the case. Even if he could feel the frustrations from the meeting that were so thick you could almost cut through them with a knife, Neil was sure that the unsub would not get away with this. Most serial killers either got sloppy, unlucky, ran out of steam or were upended through strong police work. He was always betting on the latter when push came to shove, as there was no stronger motivation for those in law enforcement than putting an end to a serial killer or mass crimes of violence. Whatever it took. There would be no difference here.

The fact that Paula was spearheading the investigation, along with Gayle, gave Neil the confidence that, with his help, and the advances in forensics and digital technology, it was only a matter of time before the unsub was apprehended.

And it couldn't come soon enough for female professors.

On Tenth Street in a low-income part of town, Neil pulled his car up behind a red Jeep Wagoneer. He could see a man behind the wheel but couldn't identify him. Reaching for the ATF-issued Glock 47 Gen5 MOS 9x19mm pistol in his duty holster, Neil wondered if he would need to use it. Those tensions lessened when he watched a husky man with messy brown shoulder-length hair, parted on the left side, and a beardstache, emerge from the Jeep, and Neil recognized him as Agent Vinny Ortiz. The thirty-five-year-old Hispanic divorced dad had worked in undercover assignments for the past four years, successfully meandering between risky operations involving arson, explosives and illegal firearms. It had played havoc with his love life, though Neil knew that Ortiz was currently romantically involved with an international flight attendant.

Putting his gun away, Neil waited for Ortiz to get into the passenger seat. Once he did, Neil said cautiously, "Hey. Everything okay?"

"Yeah, I'm fine," Ortiz said, running a hand across his mouth. "Took me a minute to get away without being noticed, if you know what I mean."

"I do." Neil understood fully just how risky the covert work was, having gone undercover himself a time or two during his career with the ATF. He certainly didn't want to jeopardize the operation. But Ortiz's safety was even more important. "What do you have for me?" Neil asked him.

"The arms trafficking operation is on," Ortiz replied in no uncertain terms. "The gunrunner, Craig Eckart, is setting up shop in Rendall Cove, using the dark web as a back door to collect and traffic in contraband firearms and ammunition, as well as gun trafficking in our own neck of the woods. Berettas, Glocks, Hi-Point, Uzis, Walthers, you name it."

"Yeah, I gathered as much." Neil considered the intel he had picked up on Craig Eckart, a forty-five-year-old who'd presented himself as a legal gun dealer and internet businessman, while operating on the fringes in his criminal enterprises. Though his legitimate interests had proven to be a good cover, selling guns and ammo on the black market had proven to be far more profitable. But if this didn't go south, they would soon be putting Eckart out of business, once and for all.

"I've set myself up as a buyer," Ortiz said, "promising to bring in loads of cash and a distribution system to kill for, figuratively speaking, both domestically and abroad."

"Good." Neil grinned at his ability to remain poised and use humor in the face of danger. He knew that the ATF was willing to front the money needed with a bigger payout in return, in breaking up the arms-dealing network. "When is this going to go down?"

"Soon," the agent promised. "I need a bit more time to ingratiate myself with Eckart, ever wary, and his goons, then we should be all set to blow this thing wide open."

"Okay." Neil regarded him. "If you ever get the sense that they're on to you, get out of there in a hurry and we'll do what we need to."

"I will." Ortiz jutted his chin. "You know me. I try to stay two steps ahead, at least, while watching my back at every turn."

"I get that." Neil nodded. "I also believe you can never be too careful. If you're ever in trouble, you know where to reach me."

"Back at you," Ortiz said, meeting his gaze. "Heard from one of the guys in the FIU with the Rendall Cove PD that you were getting involved in the Campus Killer investigation."

"I was asked to come on as a profiler," Neil acknowledged, "in hopes of nailing the unsub before anyone else gets killed."

"Good luck with that. A serial killer on the loose is bad for everyone, including Craig Eckart, who's been living with a professor, Laurelyn Wong, when he's not dirty dealing."

"Hmm… Interesting." Neil reacted to the irony. "Does she know about him as a gunrunner?"

"I don't think so," Ortiz indicated. "Eckart seems to have her totally fooled as Mr. Nice Guy."

"Could Eckart be responsible for the serial killings?"

Neil wondered seriously. "Perhaps as a deadly diversion to his arms trafficking?"

"I doubt it. In my opinion, we're talking about two lanes here. I've been watching Eckart like a hawk for weeks now and, though he's deadly in his own right in pushing contraband small arms and ammo, leading to gun deaths around the world, I don't see him masquerading on the side as a serial killer. Wouldn't be very good for business with law enforcement on the case stepping into his space, with Eckart's full knowledge that he's in the hot seat. As opposed to what he's not privy to," Ortiz added in reference to his undercover assignment.

"Maybe you're right." Neil gave the gunrunner the benefit of the doubt, knowing that they were angling at the moment for the unsub picked up on surveillance video that likely wasn't Craig Eckart. Particularly with Ortiz shadowing his every move.

"Anyway, hope you nail the son of a bitch," the undercover agent said. "Soon."

"Yeah," Neil muttered. "Back at you."

"That's the plan, right?" Ortiz ran a hand through his hair. "I better go."

"Okay." Neil certainly didn't want his cover to be blown. Or his life endangered any more than it already was. "Talk to you soon."

Ortiz nodded and left the car. Neil watched as he got back in the Jeep and drove off. He followed suit, detouring in a different direction as Neil headed home, his mind on the dual investigations he was now part of.

BLANES TAVERN WAS on Mack Road and already pretty busy by the time Paula arrived with Gayle in separate cars. They sat together, separate from colleagues, and ordered organic beer. For her part, Paula wished Neil could have joined them. But he was otherwise engaged. Maybe next time. She wasn't about to allow herself to get too attached to the visiting professor—who may or may not have been single—even if she felt comfortable conversing with him.

Gayle broke into her thoughts by asking, while holding a mug, "So, what do you make of Professor Ramirez's observations about our Campus Killer unsub?"

"He nailed it," Paula decided, based on what she already knew about serial killers, thanks in part to her former husband and his siblings in law enforcement. "Or at least he certainly seems to know what he's talking about in characterizing the unsub and what we need to look for in our search."

"I agree. His perspective can certainly aide the cause in knowing what we're likely up against."

"Yes, it can." Paula tasted the beer.

"Doesn't hurt matters any that the man's hot," Gayle remarked.

"True." It was something Paula could not deny one bit. She regarded the detective, who had recently ended a long relationship and almost immediately jumped back in the ring. Was she angling for Neil?

"Unfortunately, he's not my type," Gayle said, as if reading her mind. "Seems more like yours."

"You think?" Paula blushed.

"Based on what you've told me you look for in a man, definitely." Gayle sipped her beer. "Whether or not he's available is another matter. If you're interested, maybe you should find out."

"We'll see." Paula was noncommittal as to whether or not to go down that road. "My divorce is still relatively recent, so I have to tread carefully in putting myself out there again."

"I understand. But a year is an awfully long time to do without. I'm just saying, if you know what I mean," Gayle said with an amused grin.

"I think I do." Paula laughed at her brazen nature. "Still, I can wait till the right guy comes along, whoever that might be."

"Okay." Gayle tasted more beer. "Speaking of Agent Ramirez, I learned from the guys in the department's Firearms Investigation Unit that he and the ATF are working on a major illegal weapons probe."

Paula cocked a brow. "Really?"

"Yep. From what I understand, it's international in scope." She grabbed a handful of peanuts from a bowl on the table. "Not too surprising that the visiting professor can walk and chew gum at the same time, to coin a phrase."

"That he can, and then some," Paula concurred, while curious about the arms investigation and even more so about other aspects of his life. "We'll take whatever Agent Ramirez can send our way in the Campus Killer investigation."

"Amen to that." Gayle laughed and popped a couple of peanuts in her mouth. "So, how's your friend doing on her vacation on Maui?"

"Having a ball." Paula was mindful that Gayle grew up on the Hawaiian island and lived on Oahu as well, in Honolulu, before she relocated to the mainland and

Michigan a decade ago. "She can't seem to get enough of working on her tan and sipping piña coladas."

Gayle gave a chuckle. "Sounds like she has the Hawaii fever."

"I think so." Paula grinned and grabbed some peanuts, while wondering when a fever for stepping out of her comfort zone would overtake her.

When she got home an hour later, Paula watched as Chloe jumped off a chair and rubbed against her leg. She giggled. "Show the love," she teased her.

After feeding the cat, Paula phoned her sorority sister and former college roommate, Josie Woods, knowing that while on vacation with her latest boyfriend, Rob, Josie was on Hawaii time, which was six hours behind Michigan time.

Josie accepted the video chat request, appearing on the small cell phone screen as Paula stood by the window in the great room. The thirty-five-year-old senior analyst for a Wall Street firm was attractive and green-eyed, with long, straight brown hair and curtain bangs. She broke into a big smile. "Aloha!"

"Aloha." Paula grinned. "Hope I didn't catch you at a bad time?"

"You didn't. Rob's out for a game of golf on a Ka'anapali course, leaving me all by my lonesome to soak up the afternoon sun."

Paula laughed. "I can see that." She could tell that Josie was lounging on a beach chair beneath an umbrella on the West Maui coastline, while wearing a red tankini.

"Wish you were here," Josie told her.

"Me too." Paula was envious, having never been to Hawaii. Between Josie and Gayle singing its praises, this was something she hoped to rectify. "Maybe someday I'll hop on a plane and check out Maui and the other Hawaiian Islands for myself."

"You should. It's like no other place on Earth."

"Hmm…" Paula didn't doubt that. But visiting it alone might not be half as enjoyable as being in the company of a romantic partner. She wondered if Neil had ever been to Hawaii. The thought that he might well have taken another woman to paradise somehow ruined the fantasy, which Paula felt she had no right to have at this stage, if ever.

"Imagine what trouble we could get into if we went together." Josie broke into her reverie.

"That's what I'm afraid of." Paula giggled and watched as Chloe came over to her, as if jealous that she was being ignored.

"I'm sure you'd keep us on the straight and narrow at the end of the day, Detective Lynley," Josie quipped.

"Absolutely," Paula concurred, as her mind turned to the current serial killer case and where it might be headed with Neil on board as part of the task force.

WITH HER LEGS folded beneath her, Gayle Yamasaki sat on a faux-leather love seat in the living room of her Pine Street town house, watching cable television. Or trying to anyway. Her mind was elsewhere. Weighing heavily on it was her latest case. Having a serial killer in their midst, terrorizing females who happened to be teaching at Addison University, wasn't exactly what she'd signed up for when joining the Rendall Cove Police Department ten years ago. Or even, for that matter, when she'd been promoted to the Detective Bureau six years later. Both had followed her time as a detective with the Honolulu Police Department, once she'd graduated from the University of Hawai'i Maui College with an Associate in Applied Sciences Degree in Administration of Justice.

But, then again, no one she currently worked with wanted to be going after the so-called Campus Killer. Not that they had much choice. The unsub was still at large and needed to be stopped. As the lead detective in the investigation—at least for the two murders that occurred within the city limits outside the college—she felt the pressure to solve this case. With time being of the essence.

Gayle knew that the same was true for Paula Lynley, her detective sergeant friend who headed the university's Department of Police and Public Safety probe into the murders, with two occurring on campus. Together, along with their task force, Gayle hoped one thing led to another in putting the brakes on the unsub's homicidal tendencies before they got totally out of hand.

Having Professor Neil Ramirez on board as a criminal profiler might be just what they needed to unmask the perpetrator. The handsome ATF special agent was equally important to the Rendall Cove PD's Firearms Investigation Unit for his role in the joint investigation into the sale and distribution of illegal arms. Based on what she'd heard about him, she felt that Agent Ramirez was up to the challenge of juggling his multiple assignments without missing a beat.

Gayle's thoughts shifted back to the Campus Killer investigation. Or more specifically, one of the detectives working the case for the DPPS, Michael Davenport. Honestly, she had the biggest crush on him. Definitely her type. Too bad he was a happily married family man. Or was that only a facade?

Not that she wanted to test the waters, even if tempting. Yes, she was single again after her last serious relationship fell apart. And she'd started dating again. But she knew where to draw the line. Davenport was nice to be around, but that was it. She would turn her attention elsewhere as it related to romance.

Gayle grabbed the remote to turn off the big-screen television. She unfolded her legs and stood up, her bare feet feeling the cold of the hardwood flooring, and headed upstairs for bed.

ON FRIDAY MORNING, Paula tied her hair in a short ponytail and threw on a black tank top, pink high-rise leggings and black-and-white running sneakers for a quick jog in Rendall Creek Park before work. Though Paula had found it to be a safe place to run, or otherwise spend time in the forested setting with plenty of trails and great scenery, mindful of the serial killer at large, she had begun bringing along her SIG Sauer pistol. She kept it in an ankle holster, but she'd have no trouble grabbing it quickly, if needed, to defend herself. Beyond that, she had taken some classes in Krav Maga, a method of self-defense comprising a combo of such techniques as boxing, karate, judo and even wrestling.

I've never had to put it in practice, knock on wood, Paula told herself, as she started her jaunt though the eastern white pines and maple trees and thick shrubbery in the park. She spotted a squirrel or two, along with some robins and sparrows, none of which seemed to pay her much mind.

She had just begun to get into a comfortable groove when Paula heard footsteps behind her. They seemed to be growing closer, even as she sought to put some distance between her and the runner. With her heart pounding, as much due to the rise in her heart rate from jogging as an overactive imagination in being brazenly attacked by the Campus Killer, Paula was determined not to go down without a fight. Instincts kicked in, and she mentally prepared to grab her firearm and whip around to face her assailant, even while continuing to move forward. Though she had no reason to believe that she had suddenly gone from a detective hunting the unsub to becoming a target of the killer, Paula was taking no chances in having her life cut short.

Just as she slowed her movement, bent down and removed the SIG Sauer pistol, Paula heard a familiar voice say in an ill at ease tone, "Paula…?"

Having already been in the process of turning and pointing the barrel of her gun at him, she gazed into the intense gray-brown eyes of Neil Ramirez. He came to a screeching halt, close enough to kiss her, before taking an involuntary step backward, with the SIG Sauer separating them.

Raising his hands in mock surrender, Neil said, wide-eyed, "Whoa! Don't shoot. You've got me, Detective Lynley."

I do, at that, Paula mused, still gripping the pistol firmly, but lowering it ever so cautiously. "Neil. You startled me!"

"My apologies," he asserted. "Didn't mean to come up on you like that. Guess I was caught up in my own thoughts."

Or was that a convenient excuse? Paula asked herself. She held his gaze. "Are you following me?" Her first thought was that perhaps he was doing so as another secret assignment, in protecting her from a serial killer, while part of the joint task force. But, if so, wouldn't her boss, Shailene McNamara, have told her?

"Wish I could say that were true, in the nicest way, of course," he answered, an amused grin playing on his lips. "As it is, I just happened to be out for a run, like you. Believe me, I'm just as surprised to see you as you clearly are to see me. I assure you that our nearly running into one another was purely happenstance. Nothing more."

"Oh, really?" Paula was still a little suspicious but knew it was totally unwarranted. Even if unexpected. She gave him a once-over and could see that, like her, he was dressed for a run, wearing a black workout jersey, gray jogger pants and black running sneakers. His muscular long arms had her imagining being wrapped in them. "So, you live around here?" she asked curiously.

"Right across the street from the park," he explained. "I'm renting a nice little house while I'm in town." He paused. "Where are you?"

"I live a block away," she told him, knowing he could easily have found out for himself, had he been interested.

"I see. So we're neighbors?"

"I suppose." The idea of having him so proximate did admittedly have its appeal.

He brought his arms down and peered at her gun, still halfway raised. "You want to put that thing away?"

"Yes, sorry." Embarrassed that she had held on to it as long as she had, Paula stuffed the pistol back into its holster. "Guess I'm just a bit spooked these days, with a serial killer on the loose."

"Perfectly understandable." Neil's voice was soothing. "Better safe than sorry, right?"

"Right." She flashed her teeth and said, "Better get back to it."

"Care for some company?"

"Yes, I'm up for a running partner who can keep up with me," Paula expressed boldly.

"Sounds like a challenge." Neil laughed. "I'll try my best not to disappoint."

Something told her there was little chance of that. She put him to the test anyway, breaking away speedily, only to see him catch up with little to no effort at all. "Do you run at the park often?" she wondered, while acknowledging that it was entirely possible that they had simply missed each other previously.

"Not so often," he told her. "I usually try to get in a short run on campus between classes, given all the inviting paths with lots of scenery for distractions. How about you?"

"I run in the park maybe three times a week and go to the gym once a week," Paula added, as if she needed to prove her fitness.

"Good for you. Haven't gotten to the gym yet since I've been in town, but I try to work out whenever I can."

"Could've fooled me," Paula teased him, needing only to get one look at the man as a physical specimen to know that he was in tip-top shape. "I'm sure that comes often enough."

Neil chuckled. "Ditto. You obviously know what it takes to maintain an amazing physique, from what I can see."

She blushed. "Back at you."

He grinned. "So, how was the outing after the task force meeting?"

"Good," she said. "Just drinks and conversation, before everyone went home for the night." Paula eyed him. "How did you make out with your plans for the evening?" Did she truly want to know if he was with another woman?

"Good," he answered vaguely. "Just had something I needed to tend to."

So, he doesn't want to elaborate, she thought. Maybe that was a good thing. "I bought a copy of your book."

"Really?" He lifted a brow.

"Yes, and read the entire thing in one sitting," Paula admitted, at the risk of giving him a big head. "It was quite interesting in giving a deeper perspective on criminal profiling."

"Glad you were able to pick up something from it," Neil said, wiping perspiration from his brow with the back of his hand. "You never know how much will register and how much won't."

"It registered," she assured him. "As did what you had to say during the task force meeting."

"Good." He grinned sideways. "I really do want to help in any way I can to bring this unsub to justice. Or at least give you more to work with in delving into his psyche as a serial killer."

She nodded. "You're succeeding on both fronts."

Abruptly, Paula raced him to the clearing, beating him by a fraction, though suspecting he had let her win this time. As they caught their breaths, laughing like being in on a good joke, she suddenly decided to kiss him. Cupping Neil's chiseled cheeks, she just laid a big one on his mouth, which he returned in kind till Paula unlocked their lips, feeling embarrassed at her unusual boldness. Yet she wasn't at all sorry she did it.

"Sorry about that," she apologized nevertheless. "It was just something I wanted to do and went for it."

"Nothing to be sorry about." Neil grinned out of one corner of his mouth. "Happens to the best of us. And it was a nice kiss at that."

Though she didn't disagree in the slightest, Paula felt this probably wasn't the best moment to go down this road. So, she told him awkwardly, "Uh, this is where I head home. I have to go get ready for work."

"Okay." He met her eyes, but his own were unreadable. Was that good or bad?

"I'll see you later." She turned away and started to jog down the sidewalk, almost expecting Neil to follow, as if he had nothing better to do.

It never happened, leaving Paula to ponder the kiss and the man himself alone.

Chapter Five

Neil welcomed a hot shower after his run, but felt his temperature rise while thinking about the unanticipated kiss from Paula. Her full lips were as soft as cotton and contoured perfectly with his own. He'd be lying if he said the thought of kissing her hadn't crossed his mind once or twice. Hell, even more than that. But she had beaten him to the punch, indicating they were on the same wavelength.

Then Paula had hastily left him hanging, even if understandable that she, like him, still had another workday to prepare for. Neil could only wonder where they went from here. Or had her divorce made Paula more squeamish when it came to anything more than a quick kiss before a goodbye?

After dressing and having a quick bowl of cereal to go with a strong cup of coffee, Neil dropped by his office at the college, picked up the exams for his first class and went to it. Waiting for him there, before the undergraduate students began to pour in, was Desmond Isaac, a twenty-five-year-old graduate teaching assistant.

Working on a Master of Arts in Criminal Justice, Desmond was about his height and more on the slender side, with dark blond hair in a layered men's bob and a chin puff goatee. Behind retro glasses were blue eyes. "Hey," he said casually.

"Hey." Neil sat his briefcase on the desk and opened it. "Brought something for you." He handed him the exams, which Desmond would soon be handing out and collecting from the students.

"Think they're up to the challenge?" Desmond joked.

"If not, then I haven't been doing my job very well."

"We both know that's not true. Seems like you have them eating out of your hands."

Neil laughed. "Don't know if I'd go quite that far. But I am here to teach what I can."

"Speaking of which, I heard that you're working with the Department of Police and Public Safety in trying to identify and flush out the Campus Killer."

"Word travels fast," Neil quipped, though not at all surprised, as the school newspaper had picked it up. "I'm offering my thoughts on what—and whom—the authorities investigating the case are up against," he said, downplaying his credentials as a criminal profiler.

"Well, it's smart of them to take advantage of your presence on campus," Desmond told him. "We'll all be a lot better off when this serial killer nightmare is over."

"I hear you." Neil spotted students beginning to file in. "Right now, let's see if we can get the next generation of law enforcement personnel to pass my class and graduate."

"Yeah. There is that hurdle they need to climb." Desmond dangled the multiple-choice tests in his hand.

Neil greeted students, while also collecting their cell phones to be returned after the exam. "Good morning," he said routinely, often getting in return, "Morning, Professor Ramirez." He was still trying to get used to being seen as a visiting professor instead of an ATF special agent. Could the former replace the latter as a more permanent thing?

He honed in on one student, in particular, named Roger Woodward. The twenty-two-year-old senior and honors student stood out because of his rainbow-colored gelled Mohawk hairstyle, lanky frame and dark eyes. Neil saw him as one of his smartest students, who had indicated a strong interest in working for the Bureau of Alcohol, Tobacco, Firearms and Explosives. He grinned at Roger and said, "Good luck with the exam."

"Thanks," Roger said, a crooked smile on his lips.

Not that Neil thought he needed any luck acing the test. This common, but useful for some, phrase was passed along to other students that Neil engaged, with Desmond following suit.

THE KISS THAT landed on Neil Ramirez's firm lips was admittedly still on Paula's mind as she pulled up to the two-story Tudor home on Winsome Road in Rendall Cove that Odette Furillo had owned with her estranged husband, Allen Furillo. Paula had been trying to speak with him since his wife was murdered, but the man had seemingly kept them running around in circles. Till now. Furillo had requested the meeting, while making it clear that he didn't need to have a lawyer present. That by no means made Paula believe he had nothing to do with the murder, but at the very least suggested that he wanted to give that appearance.

Exiting her car, she noted the blue Dodge Charger parked in the driveway. Paula knew that a white Honda

Insight belonging to Odette Furillo that she'd driven to the campus was still being processed for possible evidence in a homicide. Paula's sidearm was tucked away in her gun holster but could be quickly accessed, if needed. The thought of pointing it at Neil this morning crossed her mind, causing her to blush as the potential threat had turned out to be the ATF agent turned visiting professor, whom she wound up kissing instead of killing.

I need to not be so jumpy in the future, Paula mused. At least where it pertained to Neil. But when it came to the Campus Killer, all bets were off.

Before she could ring the doorbell, the door swung open. Standing there was a medium-sized, short man in his midthirties with dark hair in an undercut fade and blue eyes. Paula showed her badge and said, "Detective Lynley. Are you Allen Furillo?"

"Yeah, that's me," he muttered. "Come in."

She followed him inside and took a sweeping glance around at the traditional furnishings and gray carpeting.

"Would you like something to drink?" Furillo asked her.

Glancing at some empty beer cans on the kitchen counter, Paula wasn't sure if he was referring to alcoholic beverages or not. Either way, she passed. But she did agree to sit on an accent chair, while he sat across from her on a sofa, so she could keep her eye on him. "We've been wanting to talk to you about your wife's death…"

"I know. I just needed some time to clear my head before speaking with anyone," he said, lowering his eyes. "The way Odette died really shook me."

"I understand that you and your wife were separated,"

Paula pointed out, not yet willing to give him the benefit of any doubt. "What was that all about?"

"That was her choice, not mine." Furillo pursed his lips. "I wanted to try and make the marriage work, even if we had trouble seeing eye to eye of late. But she wasn't interested in that and asked me to leave. I did, but still hoped she might come to her senses, before it was too late."

Paula peered at him and asked bluntly, "Did you kill your wife, Mr. Furillo?"

"No, I could never have done such a horrible thing," he asserted. "I loved Odette."

Isn't that what most say before and after killing their spouses? Paula thought. "I need to know where you were the night your wife was murdered," she demanded, supplying him with the estimated time frame.

Squaring his shoulders, Furillo responded straightforwardly, "I was at work as a warehouse picker on the afternoon shift at a distribution center on Hackett Road. Didn't leave till after midnight. Plenty of other workers saw me. You can check."

If true, Paula knew this would mean he couldn't have been at his wife's office on campus during the time of her death. "I'll do that," she promised. She regarded him directly. "Do you know of anyone who may have wanted to harm your wife?" Paula didn't discount that the unsub could have targeted a specific victim and added the others for effect, and to throw them off his trail.

Furillo's brow furrowed. "Maybe the man Odette decided to give her affections to."

Paula narrowed her eyes. "Are you saying your wife was having an affair?"

"Yeah, she was." His voice thickened. "Hard as it is

for me to come to terms with, even if she believed our marriage was over."

"Do you know the name of this other man?" Paula asked interestedly.

"Yeah. His name is Joseph Upton. He worked with her as a professor in the mathematics department at the university," Furillo muttered glumly. "He could've killed her if Odette had a change of heart and wanted to come back to me."

"I'll have a chat with Professor Upton," Paula promised, while wondering if Odette Furillo might have done a reverse course. Or had her relationship with her husband been doomed either way? Paula understood all too well that was inevitable in some marriages.

She asked Furillo a few questions about the other victims attributed to the Campus Killer and decided that it was unlikely that he had anything to do with their deaths.

"HE CAME IN VOLUNTARILY," Mike Davenport told Paula an hour later, as they looked at the video monitor of Professor of Mathematics Joseph Upton sitting in an interview room in the Department of Police and Public Safety.

"Smart move on his part," she uttered, after an attempt to reach Upton had come up short. Paula studied the professor, who was white, blue-eyed, fit and in his late thirties, with jet-black hair worn in a short pompadour cut.

"There's more," Davenport indicated. "Upton says he's the man in the surveillance video from outside the Gotley Building that we released to the media."

"Really?" Paula eyed the professor again and wondered if he was there to confess to killing his lover. "I'd better get in there and see what he has to say."

"Let me know if you need backup on this one."

"Okay." She headed into the room, where the suspect sat in a metal chair at a square wooden table. "Joseph Upton, I'm Detective Lynley. Mind telling me what you're doing here?" She decided to be coy about it.

Fidgeting, he responded, "To talk about Odette Furillo."

Paula sat across from him and advised that the conversation was being video recorded, having hit the switch to activate it on the way in. "What about her?"

"Odette and I were having an affair," he said thoughtfully.

"For how long?" Paula wondered.

"A few months." He paused. "But it wasn't just about sex. We were in love, and she was preparing to file for divorce."

Paula peered across the table. "But that never happened..."

Upton lowered his head. "I know she was murdered... and that security video showed someone fleeing the building where Odette and I had our offices." He drew a breath. "That was me," he repeated what had already been told to Davenport.

"Are you saying you murdered Professor Furillo?" Paula asked point-blank.

He lifted his eyes and met hers unblinkingly and said firmly, "No, I didn't kill her. But I saw Odette in her office, where we were supposed to meet." He sighed. "She was dead. Someone had killed her."

"Did you call 911?" Paula asked skeptically.

"No."

"Why not?"

"I don't know," he claimed. "Guess I panicked, not knowing if the killer was still on the floor. Or if I would be blamed for what happened. Not thinking clearly, I just took off, knowing there was nothing I could do to save Odette. It was too late for that."

Paula didn't disagree, per se, based on the autopsy report. But who knew for certain, had he acted promptly? "Did you see anyone else coming or leaving the building?" she pressed him.

"No." Upton's brows knitted. "There were other people outside, going about their business and whatnot, but I was in too much of a hurry to get away, so I never really focused on anyone else. Sorry."

"How did you get to the Gotley Building in the first place?" Paula asked, knowing it was centrally located on campus, but not usually walkable.

"I drove," he admitted. "But I didn't want to go to my car, fearing it would be seen on surveillance video, so I ran off and came back for it in the morning. As I said, I panicked. I know it was an unwise thing to do. When I saw the video footage on my tablet, I recognized myself and knew it was only a matter of time before someone else did. So…here I am—"

She glanced at the camera and wondered what Davenport thought. For her part, Paula felt the professor's story was credible, if not suspicious and sad at the same time. "Would you be willing to submit a DNA sample?" she asked him.

Upton hedged, but then responded as if having an epiphany, "Yes, since I have nothing to hide insofar as what happened to Odette."

That remains to be seen, Paula thought, but welcomed

the opportunity to collect his DNA to see if there was a match with the unidentified DNA profile scraped from underneath Odette Furillo's fingernails. There would be more questions for Joseph Upton down the line, but this was certainly a good step forward in seeing whether he was a killer. Or a misguided former lover to a dead woman.

Twenty minutes later in her office, Paula made the same observation to Davenport, while they awaited the DNA results. "My gut tells me that Upton did not kill Professor Furillo. Much less the other professors."

"You're probably right," the detective concurred, frowning. "The unsub likely wouldn't have been as sloppy in his comings and goings, based on the trajectory of the other killings attributed to the Campus Killer."

"Upton almost certainly contaminated the crime scene," she complained.

"As did Joan McCashin, the student and presumably first to arrive at the scene that morning," he observed. "That notwithstanding, and even if it turns out that Upton isn't our unsub, we still have enough to work with in moving ahead."

Paula did not disagree. "If Upton's on the level, his own life might have been spared," she contended, "had the unsub stuck around long enough to make sure there were no living witnesses to the perp's criminality."

"You're right." Davenport twisted his lips. "In this case, timing does seem to be everything. The killer is using it to his advantage. But that won't last forever."

"It had better not." She frowned at the thought, with a serial monster undoubtedly still hungry for more victims.

As THE NOON hour approached and turned into 1:00 p.m., Neil wondered if Paula was free for lunch. If she was like him, she probably passed this up often when in the heat of an investigation. On the other hand, a person had to eat sometime. He hoped this would be a chance to get to know one another better.

He was in his office when he phoned her. "Hey," he said when she answered, the thought of that kiss immediately entering his head.

"Hey." She left it at that.

"If you're not busy and haven't eaten yet, I was wondering if you'd like to join me for lunch?" Neil didn't want to spook her by calling it a date, in case that wasn't something she was open to right now. "We can talk shop and—"

"Yes, I'd be happy to meet you for lunch," Paula broke in enthusiastically. "Where?"

"I thought we could eat at the Union Building food court," he suggested, as a neutral spot.

"Sounds perfect. I can be there in five minutes."

"See you then." Neil disconnected and found himself excited at the prospect of seeing the lovely detective in mere minutes. He conferred briefly with his TA, Desmond Isaac, who would be grading the exams and either putting smiles or frowns on the faces of students, before heading out of the building.

In his Chevy Suburban SUV, Neil drove across campus to the Union Building on Bogle Lane. He parked in the lot and went inside to the food court, where he was surprised to see that Paula was already there.

He grinned. "Hope I didn't keep you waiting too long," he kidded.

"Maybe just a bit," she tossed back at him lightheartedly. "But I'll live."

Neil laughed. "That's good to know."

They found a table, and he went with the mac and cheese, while Paula settled for street-style nachos. Both had coffee.

Rather than get back to the kiss and what it could potentially mean, Neil asked casually, "Any news on the investigation?"

Paula, who had been deep in thought while eating, looked at him and said, "As a matter of fact, there has been some…"

"Oh?" He met her eyes curiously.

"The man seen in the surveillance video at the Gotley Building has been identified as Joseph Upton, a mathematics professor," she informed him. "Who also happened to be the lover of Odette Furillo."

"Really?" Neil knew she was estranged from her husband. But still.

"Yep. Upton came in voluntarily and admitted to coming upon Professor Furillo's body, after making plans to meet in her office." Paula dabbed a napkin to her mouth. "He says he panicked and fled the scene without calling 911."

"Did you believe him?" Neil asked.

"Honestly, I was on the fence there, but he agreed to supply a sample of his DNA."

"And…?"

"Upton's DNA didn't match the unidentified sample collected from beneath Odette's nails." Paula furrowed her brow. "Apart from leaving the scene of a crime, there was no reason to believe he's the unsub."

"Makes sense." Neil scooped up some macaroni and cheese on a fork. "What about the husband?"

She poked at her nachos. "Allen Furillo has a solid alibi for the time frame in which his wife was murdered. He couldn't have done it."

"Can't say I'm too surprised in either instance," Neil remarked thoughtfully. "As victim number four of the so-called Campus Killer, Odette Furillo most likely wasn't intimately connected to her murderer as much as the unsub could have been to the first or second victim—then moved beyond that, were it the case, in the subsequent killings."

"Sounds logical, coming from a profiler," Paula agreed. "Of course, as a crime investigator, we can't afford to leave any stones unturned."

"Wouldn't expect you to." Neil sat back in the chair and lifted his coffee cup. "Until you get the guy, no one's above suspicion. Nor should anyone be."

She smiled. "I figured we'd see eye to eye on this."

And even more, he thought, tasting the coffee and grinning at her. "Absolutely."

Paula lifted her own cup in thought. "As for going after bad elements, I hear that you're working with the Rendall Cove PD on an arms investigation."

Neil wasn't at all surprised that information flowed back and forth between the DPPS's Investigative Division and the city police department's Firearms Investigation Unit, given that they typically worked hand in hand on cases with common ground. Consequently, he didn't try to dance his way around this. Even if, technically speaking, he needed to keep a low profile on the case while it was at a near tipping point.

"Yes," he confessed without elaborating.

"I see." She met his eyes musingly. "Is that the real reason you're in Rendall Cove?"

Neil thought about his friend and late fellow ATF agent, Ramone Munoz. And then his ex-girlfriend, Constance Chen, who turned Neil's life upside down. Locking his eyes with Paula's steady gaze, he told her straightforwardly, "Not exactly."

Chapter Six

It occurred to Paula that perhaps Neil was on a mission that she was not supposed to pry about. Even if they were on the same team in her serial killer investigation. Or was there something more to his taking a position at the university as a visiting professor?

"Sorry if I've overstepped," she put out, after nibbling on more of her nachos.

"You didn't," he insisted, flashing her a small grin. "You're entitled." He paused. "I can't really talk about the ongoing arms investigation, other than to say it's what the ATF does, and sometimes with help from its partners in law enforcement."

So, there's obviously a big operation going down, Paula told herself. One she was not entitled to be privy to, in spite of working with him as a profiler in a separate case. "I understand," she said tactfully.

Neil rubbed his jawline. "Apart from that, I took the position as a visiting professor as a needed getaway from the life I had…" He pressed his hands together. "Last year, a good friend of mine, ATF Special Agent Ramone Munoz, was ambushed during an ATF Special Response Team raid on a drug trafficking compound. He was killed in the process, leaving behind a wife and two little girls. The entire thing shook me up like I'd never been before."

Paula was almost speechless in hearing the shocking details of Agent Munoz's death and its aftermath, having already learned the basics about the mission gone awry. "I'm so sorry," she managed.

"Me too." Neil stared at the remnants of his macaroni and cheese. "Ramone deserved a hell of a lot better than he got as a dedicated ATF agent. But it is what it is and I have to accept that, no matter how difficult."

"These things can take time…" Paula resisted the desire to reach across the table and touch his hand. "And there's no hurry." She sensed there was more to his story.

He nodded and met her eyes musingly. "A few months back, I was in a relationship with an anthropologist named Constance Chen. She dumped me for another guy, without giving me a good reason, and I needed to come to terms with this as well. Putting some distance between me and Constance seemed like a good idea. Along with taking a break when it came to romance."

"I'm sorry that happened to you." Paula meant every word of it. Even if in the process, it told her that he was, apparently, not seeing anyone. She felt like jumping for joy that he was available, but wondered if this was true. Perhaps in guarding his heart, he wasn't looking to jump back into a relationship any time soon.

"It was probably a good thing," Neil told her in earnest. "If I'm honest about it, things had been treading in the wrong direction between us for a while. But I chose not to see it for what it was."

"I know what you mean," Paula couldn't help but say.

"What happened with your marriage?" He regarded her intently, taking the opening she had given him.

Holding his gaze, she admitted straightforwardly, "We simply ran out of steam." She tasted her coffee, which had started to get cold, knowing he wanted more from her than that. "Scott was a good man. His parents and siblings were either in law or law enforcement. In some ways, this seemed to put extra pressure on our relationship, in addition to us both being in law enforcement ourselves. Eventually, it, along with personality clashes, took its toll on the marriage and we decided to end things."

Neil tilted his head. "Any regrets?"

"There are always regrets whenever a relationship fails and you play the blame game and wonder what you might have done differently," she answered, "which I'm sure you would attest to. But if you're asking me if I still love Scott and want to get back together with him, the answer is no on both fronts. He'll always be a part of my history," Paula did not deny. "Not my future." She looked at Neil. "Does that answer your question?"

"Yes, it does." He grinned sheepishly. "And you're absolutely right. We all have regrets on past failures. But they can—and should be—a bridge to getting things right the next time. Or the time after that."

"Agreed." She smiled back at him, believing they had climbed one hurdle in getting to know one another better. Would there be more to follow?

"Do you have family?" Neil asked, sitting back while taking a sip of water.

Paula bobbed her head. "My mom lives in Georgetown, Kentucky. I lost my dad to a heart attack when I was a teenager."

"Sorry to hear that."

"It came without warning, but was quick," she told him sentimentally. "I have no siblings. What about you?"

"Just an older sister," Neil said, resting an arm on the table. "Yancy works these days as a freelance translator in Brazil. I lost my parents in different years to cancer and an accidental fall."

It was Paula's turn to tell him she was sorry, knowing how devastating it could be without one's parents. She recalled that Scott and his siblings lost their parents in a car accident and, fortunately, had each other to lean on. "Are you and your sister close?" she asked Neil.

"Yes," he replied with a smile. "Yancy's four years older, but the difference never seemed that great when we were kids. In any event, we've always had each other's back."

"That's nice to hear." Paula wished she'd had siblings to always be able to lean on. She would have to settle for her best friend, Josie, along with her ex-sister-in-law, Madison, whom Paula had remained close with since her divorce. Even better was the notion of forming a bond with someone she could share her life with.

After they left the Union Building, Neil walked Paula to her car. "Thanks for lunch," she told him, after he'd insisted on paying for it.

He nodded, grinning. "Anytime."

She waited a beat then, looking into his eyes, said, "Guess I'll catch you later."

"All right." Neil flashed her a serious look. "About that kiss…"

"What about it?" She was almost afraid to ask, her heart pounding.

He suddenly cupped her cheeks and kissed Paula on

the mouth. The kiss was powerful enough to make her go weak in the knees. Something told Paula that Neil would catch her were her legs to go out from under her.

After his lips parted from hers, his voice dropped an octave when Neil uttered soulfully, "I just wanted to let you know that the feeling of something between us is mutual."

As she caught her breath, Paula realized that he had just given them permission to try and unwrap those feelings over the course of time.

BACK AT HIS office that afternoon, Neil reflected on what he saw as a breakthrough on the connection he was starting to feel with Paula. He had no idea if it would go anywhere. Or if both of them were merely spinning their wheels in seeking to get beyond broken relationships. He, for one, was willing to put one foot in front of the other and see what happened. From the way Paula's lips contoured perfectly with his, it indicated to Neil that she was up for meeting him halfway. That was all he could ask for at this point, given that they both were in the midst of criminal investigations, occupying their time.

On his laptop, Neil contacted his sister for a video chat. He noted the minor time difference between Rendall Cove and São Paulo, Brazil, where Yancy lived with her bank manager boyfriend, Griffin Oliviera. She accepted the call and Neil watched his sister's face light up. At forty, she looked ten years younger, with dark blond hair in a medium-length A-line cut. Like him, Yancy had their father's deep gray-brown eyes.

"Hey," he said.

"Hey back, Neil."

"You busy?" Like him, he knew she worked long hours, often at the expense of quality time, in spite of being in a long-term relationship with Griffin.

"I think I can spare a few minutes for my brother," she teased him.

"Okay. Just wanted to check in with you."

"And I thank you for that." Yancy went on to bring him up to date on her current comings and goings, before he talked a bit about himself.

"So, being a professor agrees with you these days?" she asked curiously.

"Yeah, you could say that," he told her. "Still keeping my day job, though, just in case teaching blows up in my face."

"I doubt that will happen." Yancy laughed. "But at least you'll have two directions you can go in."

"That's true." *Make it three directions*, Neil considered, when it came to Paula.

As if on the same wavelength, Yancy eyed him carefully and asked, "So, how's your love life these days? Or shouldn't I ask?"

"You can ask." He grinned wryly.

"Then I'm asking. And please don't tell me you're still pining for the one who let you get away?"

"I'm not," Neil made clear. Not by a long shot. "There is someone in the picture," he told her.

"Really?" Yancy's eyes brightened. "Tell me more…"

He did, while being clear that things were still in the early stages with Paula, with neither of them knowing if, like birds, they had the wings to make this fly. But at least she was giving him something to shoot for, and vice versa.

His sister concurred and wished them both luck, while

even being presumptuous in inviting them to come for a visit to Brazil. Neil laughed, while taking that under advisement as something he could imagine happening down the line, should things progress accordingly with the nice-looking detective.

When Neil noticed that his TA had poked his head in the office, the call to Yancy was ended, with the promise to speak again soon.

"Sorry, didn't mean to interrupt," Desmond said.

"It's all right." Neil looked at him. "What's up?"

"Finished grading the exams." He stepped inside the office.

"How did they do?" Neil wondered.

"Better than expected," Desmond said. "At least for some, who aced it. Others still need to study harder to get up to snuff."

Neil nodded. "I'll have to do better to motivate them in that regard."

"You're doing a great job," the TA contended. "The onus is on them to get with the program, if they hope to graduate and move on to bigger and better things."

"Can't argue with that." Neil smiled. He was glad to see that Desmond was able and willing to keep the pressure on students to try and be the best they could be, instead of being handed life on a silver platter. Just how many students would buy into this argument remained to be seen.

"I'll send out the exam scores and wait to see how they respond," Desmond said.

"Good. I'll go over the results and see where to put greater focus," he told the TA and watched him leave. Neil then got on the phone with Doris Frankenberg, the resident agent in charge of the ATF's Grand Rapids field office, to update her on the illegal arms joint operation.

ON MONDAY MORNING, Paula was at her desk, comparing information on the four homicides credited to the Campus Killer. There appeared to be little commonality among the murder victims, per se, apart from being victimized female professors. Though this, in and of itself, showed an undeniable pattern of targeting that needed to be taken into account, there was no indication that the victims were connected otherwise in a meaningful way. This lent credence, to some degree, to the random or opportunistic theory on the crimes. But what were they missing in this equation?

There must be something, she told herself, sipping coffee, while poring over the individual case files. Her mind wandered briefly to the passionate kiss she shared with Neil the other day. The man could kiss, she established. Made her believe he could be just as great a lover. If not better. As a flicker of desire coursed through her, Paula allowed it to dissipate, filing it away for another time and place, as she put her eye back on the ball.

She went back through the cases and searched for anything that could link them together insofar as a pattern that might lead to a serial killer. Something suddenly caught her eye—or someone—as Paula honed in on the name Roger Woodward. The twenty-two-year-old senior had been questioned this summer about the murder of Debra Newton, because the associate professor had mentioned to at least one other professor that a student in her journalism class had been stalking her.

That student was identified as Roger Woodward. He

had produced an alibi and been let off the hook as a suspect in her death. Now Paula saw that Woodward, an honors student who had a dual major in journalism and criminology, had been taking a class in mathematics as an elective this semester, with Professor Odette Furillo. *Hmm, coincidence?* Paula had to ask herself. Or not?

She looked up his current class schedule and saw that Roger Woodward also happened to be taking a criminology course with Visiting Professor Neil Ramirez. One that was in session right now.

Think I'd better have a little chat with Woodward, Paula told herself. If he had something to hide, such as a pattern of serial homicides, perhaps with Neil on hand they could flush it out of the honors student together.

AFTER GOING OVER Friday's exam results without mentioning any names or grades specifically, Neil put on a good face and tried to make all the students feel as if they could talk to him if they had any trouble grasping the lectures and reading assignments. In the meantime, he would continue to do his job in the classroom as a visiting professor of criminology and hope that it was resonating to the point of motivating those in attendance to do their best in getting a good education and doing something with it.

It was about five minutes before class ended when Neil got a text message from Paula. He glanced at his cell phone, reading with interest.

One of your students, Roger Woodward, is a suspect in the Campus Killer investigation. On my way. Keep him there till I arrive.

Neil couldn't help but cock a brow with shock that someone in his class was considered a possible serial killer. He gazed at Roger Woodward, who was sandwiched in the middle row between Adriana Tilly and Fiona Liebert. Roger, not too surprisingly, had aced the exam. *He clearly got it*, Neil thought. And seemed to enjoy playing the role of amateur sleuth. Could this have evolved into becoming a real-life serial killer? He didn't seem to fit the profile. But then, profiles didn't always tell the tale where it concerned the capabilities and modus operandi of killers.

Neil turned away from him, not wanting to tip his hand that something was up. But he couldn't allow Roger to leave either. Not till Paula had questioned him and determined he was not the unsub.

Dismissing the class a little early, Neil gave them a new assignment, then casually asked Roger Woodward if he could stick around for a moment to talk about his test results.

"Yeah, sure," he responded, wide-eyed at being singled out.

After the others had left, Neil eyed him intently and said, "You did great on the exam, Roger."

"Thanks."

Neil paused. "I was asked to hold you over."

Roger looked at him warily. "By who?"

"A police detective who would like to ask you a few questions pertaining to a homicide investigation…" Neil gauged his reaction, while trying to picture one of his prized students doubling as a serial killer. Before he could respond to the question, Paula walked into the room.

"Professor Ramirez," she spoke formally. "I can take it from here…"

"Okay." Neil ceded to her authority in the matter as the lead investigator on the case, but was more than an interested observer.

Paula walked up to the student and said equably, "Roger Woodward, I'm Detective Lynley. We spoke before, during the investigation into the death of Professor Debra Newton."

"Yeah, I remember." He ran a hand nervously through his hair. "I had an alibi," he reminded her.

"You did," she conceded, "which checked out. Now I'd like to ask you about another one of your professors, Odette Furillo, who was found murdered in her office last Wednesday."

"I heard about that. Like everyone else on campus." Roger put his weight awkwardly on one foot. "What does that have to do with me?"

Paula glanced at Neil and back. "Maybe nothing. Or maybe everything."

"I don't follow," Roger said, furrowing his brow. "Are you accusing me of something?"

"Not yet." Her tone deepened. "I do find it odd though that you happened to be taking classes with two dead professors—at least one of whom you had a fixation on."

"I admit that I was attracted to Professor Newton, okay? I thought the feeling was mutual. Guess I was mistaken. But I didn't kill her and I didn't kill Professor Furillo." His nostrils flared. "Or, for that matter, the other murdered professors. I'm not this Campus Killer."

Though Neil wanted to give him the benefit of the doubt, that didn't work on the face of it when on the hunt for a serial killer. He gazed at the student and decided to get in on the questioning. "Relax, Roger. Detective Lynley is simply doing her job," Neil told him, playing the good cop, bad cop game as he regarded Paula and got her approval through an expression. "I assume you have an alibi for when Professor Furillo was murdered?" He gave him the date and time of death.

"Yeah, I do." Roger set his jaw. "I was with my girl-friend. Spent the night in her dorm room."

Paula peered at him. "Does this girlfriend have a name?"

"Last I checked," he quipped. Then Neil flashed him a stern look and Roger said, "Her name's Adriana... Adriana Tilly—"

"Adriana?" Neil said, reacting to the name of another student in his class. Like Roger, she tended to stand out with her mermaid hairstyle, featuring a blend of orange, green and red long locks with a round face. "I didn't re-alize you two were an item, and not just classmates."

"Yeah, we've been hanging out for a few weeks now," Roger stated coolly. "Been pretty much inseparable of late at night, if you know what I mean."

Neil took him at his word. "What you do and who you choose to do it with outside the classroom is your business." *So long as it doesn't involve criminal behav-ior*, he thought.

"I'll need to talk with Adriana," Paula made clear.

"Be my guest." He shifted his weight to the other foot. "She just left. If you hurry, you can probably catch her…"

Before Paula could respond, all three of them received

a text message on their cell phones. Neil regarded his and frowned as he favored Paula with a look of concern.

A bomb threat had been made at Addison University. More specifically, someone had claimed that pipe bombs had been planted at Horton Hall, the building they were currently standing in, set to detonate at any moment.

Chapter Seven

With an active bomb threat at Addison University's Horton Hall, the building was ordered evacuated immediately. A lockdown went into effect at other buildings across campus as a safety measure. Paula had been through this before. More than once. Most times, it turned out to be a false alarm. A prank that was anything but funny. This did little to quell the tension in the air, thick as fog. In the post-9/11 era, nothing could ever be taken for granted when it came to potential terroristic activities.

Not knowing if a hidden bomb could explode at any time, Paula was admittedly on pins and needles as she, along with Neil and Roger Woodward, headed hastily toward the nearest exit, followed by others. A Regional Special Response Team, which included highly trained members from the DPPS, Rendall Cove PD, Shays County Sheriff's Department, and the Bureau of Alcohol, Tobacco, Firearms and Explosives, stormed past them and entered Horton Hall tactically. They were prepared for anything they might find in trying to defuse the situation.

"Let them do their job," Neil told her firmly, as Paula had fought her instincts to want to go back inside to be in on the action in confronting the threat on campus. She knew he was right in leaving this to the RSRT.

"I will," she promised smartly, as they moved away from the building and behind barricades that had been set up. Paula took note that Roger Woodward and other students were being escorted by law enforcement to a location that had been cleared. "So, what's your take on Woodward?" she asked Neil, though having already sensed that he believed she was barking up the wrong tree with him as a suspect.

"Well, he's one of my best students. But that doesn't make him incapable of being a serial killer." Neil brushed up against her and Paula felt it down to her toes. "I don't see that here, honestly. Especially if his alibi for the first suffocation murder held up."

She considered this. "Woodward said he was at the school library at the time. A number of other students who were there verified this, more or less, though surveillance video from the library was unable to substantiate this conclusively," Paula pointed out.

"I don't see other students covering for him intentionally," Neil said doubtfully. "That includes his alibi for the latest campus killing, Adriana Tilly."

"The girlfriend student of yours," she stated knowingly.

"Afraid so." He gave her a plain look.

"I'll see if she will corroborate his story."

"If not, we'll go from there…"

Paula nodded. She liked the *we* in his words, knowing that beyond being a visiting professor, his loyalties lay with helping them get to the bottom of their serial killer investigation. Wherever it took them, on campus or off.

She lifted her eyes to his face. "Do you think this bomb threat could have anything to do with the Campus Killer case?"

Neil turned to her. "Doesn't seem likely. What would the unsub gain by diverting attention from the serial killer probe only temporarily, especially since this would be under a different set of investigators. Unless the connections put us all under the same tent in terms of a serial killer bomber."

"I was thinking the same thing," Paula told him. "We certainly wouldn't be scared off in pursuing our mission till completed, even if there were a bomber on campus. Still, it's odd that the latest threat should manifest itself at this moment in time."

"Can't argue with you there," Neil said. "But it happens. Let's just see what the RSRT comes up with, if anything."

As the situation remained tense for the next hour, they were approached by RSRT Lieutenant Corey Chamberlain. In full uniform, the tall, brawny, fortysomething man had gray hair in a military undercut. His blue eyes were narrowed as he uttered, "We located two crude homemade pipe bombs hidden on the lower level. Both have been successfully deactivated and removed from the building."

"Wow." Paula's mouth hung open for a moment at the thought of someone being killed had the bombs exploded in their presence. Herself and Neil included. "Could there be more bombs inside?"

"I don't think so," Chamberlain said. "We've done a sweep twice and come up empty, insofar as any more pipe bombs."

"What do you know, if anything, about the bomber?" Neil asked him, brows knitted.

"Still working on that. The threat was posted online to two social media sites—as if to ensure we didn't miss it." Chamberlain jutted his chin. "These were traced back to a computer in the university's main library. We have investigators and technicians at the scene examining surveillance video and collecting forensic evidence, even as we speak."

"That's good," Paula commended him. "The unsub or unsubs cannot be allowed to get away with this."

"They won't," the lieutenant assured her. "Not on my watch."

"Be sure to keep us in the loop," Neil advised Chamberlain.

"Will do." He eyed them and said thoughtfully, "If you need to go back into Horton Hall, the evacuation order has been lifted."

Paula felt relieved to know that. She imagined this was even more true for Neil, given that it housed his classroom and office. As she watched Lieutenant Chamberlain move away from them to confer with his colleagues, Neil got on his cell phone, explaining, "I need to check in with the field office on this bomb incident."

"I understand," she told him, offering a tiny smile as he put a little distance between them. She wondered just how long it would be before he had vacated the visiting professorship and moved on to other ATF duties. The idea that whatever this was between them would be short-lived disturbed her. But she had no right to expect anything lasting. Did she?

When Paula's cell phone rang, she pulled it from the

back pocket of her pants and saw that the caller was Mike Davenport. "Hey," she answered.

"Are you okay?"

"I'm fine. The situation has been neutralized."

"Glad to see that the all clear has been issued on campus," he remarked tentatively.

"Me too." Even so, Paula still felt unsettled for some reason, as if the proverbial shoe had yet to drop. "And no one got hurt, thankfully."

"Yeah. Unfortunately, we have another problem to deal with…" Davenport sighed. "Another female professor has been found dead—"

Paula's heart skipped a beat. "On campus?"

"Off," he replied tersely. "According to an officer on the scene, it looks like the same MO as the other victims of the Campus Killer."

She winced and got more info before disconnecting, only to find Neil standing right beside her. "What is it?" he asked perceptively.

Swallowing thickly, Paula told him soberly, "We have a new murder on our hands that is believed to be the work of the unsub serial killer."

THE CAMPUS KILLER celebrated his latest kill, while knowing full well that others would find it unsettling, if not downright horrific. He laughed to himself as he drove down the street, making sure he didn't go over the speed limit, drive erratically or otherwise give the cops a reason to pull him over. Were that the case, they just might be suspicious enough that he could be brought in and his carefully constructed life and living could well come tumbling down like dominoes.

Never mind the fact that he'd suffocated the good-looking professor hours ago. More than enough time to have put some distance between himself and the scene of the crime. She had been taken by surprise. Or he made it seem that way when accosting her and allowing a very false sense of security. Could he help it if she should have known not to trust anyone? Especially right now with a serial killer on the prowl.

But, like the others, she had played right into his hands like putty. And he had been more than willing to act accordingly in seeing it through. Right up until her breathing had ceased entirely and her days of teaching pesky students had come to an end. Then, like clockwork, he had left his magnificent handiwork behind for others to discover.

The Campus Killer turned left at the light, heading back onto the campus grounds—where he felt just as much at home as off campus. It made for an interesting mix while he plied his murderous trade and got away with it like this had been his destiny all along. Made him almost drool for more pretty professors to come into his grasp, before discovering there was no escape but death itself. And who knew who else might capture his fancy while he was in the mood for killing?

DETECTIVE GAYLE YAMASAKI drove her blue Ford Escape down the tree-lined Pickford Road, fretting over both the pipe bomb incident on campus and the more disturbing news that a woman had been found dead. All initial signs pointed toward this being a homicide—with the indicators sounding the Campus Killer alarm, as the victim was identified as another Addison University professor.

This can't be happening, Gayle told herself, even in the face of knowing otherwise. She had contacted Paula and Mike Davenport to this effect, warning them of the situation and agreeing to meet at the scene. Gayle pulled into the strip mall on the corner of Fulmore Street. It included a convenience store, dentist's office, shoe store and hair salon. She spotted two patrol cars, lights flashing, parked haphazardly. A male and female officer were talking to a young woman. Eyeing a corner of the small parking lot, Gayle saw that beneath an oak tree was a red Nissan Altima. A lone occupant was inside, behind the steering wheel.

After parking, Gayle checked the Smith and Wesson M&P 5.7 pistol in her custom Kydex holster and got out, approaching the officers. She flashed her identification and said, "Detective Yamasaki. What do we have?"

The twentysomething biracial female officer, who was around Gayle's height of five-five, with a black Afro puff hairstyle and brown eyes, responded glumly, "A female is deceased inside a vehicle. It appears as if she was the victim of foul play."

Gayle nodded perceptively. "We have a name?"

The male officer, who towered over them both, was in his thirties and had raven hair in a crew cut fade style and blue eyes. He answered, "Ran a make on the license plate of the Nissan Altima. It's registered to a Laurelyn Wong."

Gayle nodded and walked over to the car. The driver's side door was open. Sitting there, with the seat belt strapped across her body and wearing a floral-print midi dress, was a slender and attractive Asian female with highlighted brunette hair in a digital perm. She looked to be in her early thirties. Her head was tilted slightly to the right, eyes closed in death. A trickle of blood came down from one nostril onto her face. There was a white cotton towel with bloodstains on it, lying messily atop presumably the victim's satchel bag on the passenger seat, to suggest it was the weapon used to suffocate the victim.

A chill ran through Gayle in that moment as she stared at the woman who could very well have been an Indigenous Polynesian person like herself—telling Gayle that her own number could have come up, under other dire circumstances. She turned bleakly toward the male officer, who glanced at the other woman standing by the female officer, and said, "According to the one who discovered the body, Ms. Wong is a music professor at the university."

Gayle approached the woman, who was older than she had first thought—perhaps midthirties—and petite, with long and multilayered ombré hair, and again identified herself, "Detective Yamasaki. And you are?"

"Jeanne Roth," she told her. "I own the Roth Salon—" she pointed toward the strip mall "—over there. Professor Wong had her hair done yesterday."

"At what time?" Gayle wondered.

"Around seven p.m." Jeanne's voice shook. "She left the salon just before we closed at eight."

"Did you see Professor Wong go to her car?" Gayle cast her eyes back at the vehicle. "And was she accompanied or followed by anyone?"

"She came and left the salon alone," Jeanne responded. "I never saw anyone following her..." She took a breath. "I closed up shop and didn't notice her car till I came in this afternoon. That's when I saw Professor Wong inside, not moving, and called 911."

Gayle looked up at a nearby surveillance camera, believing it could be key to ID'ing a suspect. But the female officer threw cold water on that when she told her, "Apparently, for whatever reason, that camera isn't operational right now."

"Figures." Gayle wrinkled her nose. She could only hope that there were security cameras in the shops on the streets that might provide useful information. As she pondered this, Gayle watched Mike Davenport drive up in his white Mustang Mach-E duty vehicle. He had arrived before Paula. "Hey," Gayle said calmly as she met him halfway, while ignoring the charge she got out of being in his presence.

"Hey." He met her eyes, then glanced at the victim's vehicle. "Where are we on this?" he asked tonelessly.

As she told him and got his initial thoughts, Gayle saw that Paula, accompanied by Neil, who was driving, had pulled up. Both were undoubtedly as disturbed as she was at this latest turn of events, coming after the pipe bomb scare at the college. Though she didn't believe the two were in any way connected, Gayle kept all possibilities on the table, so long as no one had been taken into custody for either criminal act.

THE VICTIM'S NAME, Laurelyn Wong, rang a bell in Neil's head. He'd heard it before. It took a moment or two before suddenly registering. According to ATF undercover agent Vinny Ortiz, the gunrunner they were investigating, Craig Eckart, had been living with Professor Laurelyn Wong. Now she was dead—in what was all but certain a homicide and fitting the MO of the Campus Killer—and Eckart had to be considered a suspect, all things being equal involving victims acquainted with their offenders. This definitely complicated the arms trafficking case being built against the suspect.

Neil didn't shy away from that when coming clean with Paula—once he had pulled her off to the side and away from the other detectives, crime scene technicians and the chief medical examiner, all who had a part to play in the investigation. "Professor Wong may have been killed by the gun trafficker who's currently under investigation by the ATF," he told her candidly.

"Seriously?" Paula frowned. "What am I missing?"

"Just that the suspect in our arms case, Craig Eckart, was romantically involved with the professor, which was told to me recently by an undercover agent." Neil dipped his chin. "Laurelyn Wong's name stuck in my memory."

"You think she may have been involved in gun trafficking?"

"I doubt it," he contended. "The romance was likely unassociated with the illegal weapons network. But with this latest twist, Eckart could also be moonlighting as a serial killer." Though Neil had strong doubts about that, especially since Ortiz was tracking the gunrunner's movements, they had to consider all possibilities in the serial killer probe. That included those closest to the victim being involved in her death.

Paula regarded him dubiously. "Please don't tell me you want us to look the other way, with your federal case taking priority over our local investigation?"

"Actually, it's just the opposite." Neil held her gaze without blinking. "I'd like you to stay the course in your investigation, while determining one way or the other, sooner than later, if Eckart is in fact the unsub. If not, you need to take him off the suspect list, so as not to impede our ongoing arms trafficking case."

She nodded. "Understood."

"In the meantime, the fewer people who know about Craig Eckart being the subject of a federal probe, the better," Neil thought to warn her. Not that he believed for one instant that Paula would do anything reckless to jeopardize their investigation. But the same might not be true for everyone working the Campus Killer case.

"I get it." Paula touched his arm and Neil felt the warmth radiate through the sleeve of his shirt. "I, for one, will do my best not to step on your toes, Agent Ramirez, where it concerns questioning Craig Eckart about the murder of his girlfriend."

"Okay." He flashed her a grin and got one back in return, giving Neil a good feeling inside and confidence that there was something between them that needed to be explored more thoroughly.

THE VISUAL OF the latest presumed victim of an unsub serial slayer gnawed at Paula like a hideous replay of a movie she wished would just go away, as she went with Gayle to the address on Vernon Drive, where Laurelyn Wong reportedly lived with her boyfriend, Craig Eckart. In respecting Neil's wishes that Eckart be treated as only a suspect in the Campus Killer case, while not revealing that he was also the primary person of interest under federal investigation for trafficking in contraband arms and ammunition, along with other firearms-related offenses, she kept this information to herself. Once the story broke,

Gayle would learn about it from her department's Firearms Investigation Unit.

If Eckart did murder Professor Wong and the other women, he would be held fully accountable, irrespective of the federal case against him, Paula told herself determinedly, as they left the car. Passing by a silver Lincoln Navigator Reserve parked in the driveway, they headed up the walkway to the two-story American foursquare home to notify the next of kin or significant other about the professor's death.

"I hate these moments," Gayle remarked softly.

"Don't we all," Paula said, knowing that it came with the territory, no matter how painful it was having to upend the lives of the dead's loved ones. Only, in this instance, the victim's boyfriend could have more than one thing to hide in his grieving.

Gayle rang the bell, and there was the instant sound of a large dog barking inside, before it was told in a commanding voice to be quiet. A moment later, the door opened. Standing there was a tall and muscular man in his mid to late forties, with dark hair in a disheveled cut and a salt-and-pepper corporate beard.

He trained gray eyes on Paula and asked cautiously, "How can I help you?"

She showed him her ID while saying, "Detective Lynley, Investigative Division of the Department of Police and Public Safety at Addison University."

Gayle flashed her badge and said, "Detective Yamasaki, Rendall Cove PD. And you are...?"

He hesitated, then answered, "Craig Eckart. You want to tell me what this is about?"

"Maybe we should go inside," Paula suggested, while

wondering if this was where he was storing the illegal weapons. As he contemplated this, she added, "It's about Laurelyn Wong… She does live here?"

"Yeah." His mouth pursed, ill at ease.

"And what is your relationship with Ms. Wong?" Paula asked for the record.

"I'm her partner," he said matter-of-factly.

Gayle peered at him. "Can we come in?"

He nodded. The moment they stepped through the door, Paula picked up the pungent odor of marijuana. She also noted the Staffordshire bull terrier, growling threateningly, standing on all fours on bamboo flooring beside a leather sectional in the great room. Before she or Gayle needed to react, both armed, Eckart claimed, "She's harmless."

"All the same, would you mind putting your dog in another room while we talk?" Paula demanded.

"If you say so." He snickered. "C'mon, girl."

As he led the dog away, Paula glanced around at the contemporary furnishings, which may have been a facade for a criminal enterprise being investigated by the ATF. Then there was the question of multiple murders that could lead right to Craig Eckart.

When he came back into the room, Eckart eyed them back and forth and spoke bluntly, "Laurelyn's dead, isn't she?"

Gayle glanced at Paula and responded straightforwardly, "Yes. She was found in her car in a strip mall parking lot early this afternoon." Gayle paused. "She was murdered…"

Eckart's broad shoulders slumped and an expletive escaped his lips. "By that Campus Killer?"

"The investigation into Ms. Wong's death is still on-going," Paula responded simply. After a beat, she asked directly, "When did you last see her?"

He ran a hand roughly across his mouth. "Yesterday, around noon."

"That's more than twenty-four hours ago," Gayle pointed out. "Why didn't you report her missing?"

Paula knew that one could file a missing person report at any time, even if the authorities might take longer to act upon it, depending on the circumstances.

"Didn't think she was," he replied matter-of-factly. "We both have busy schedules and came and went as we pleased. It wasn't unusual for us to miss one another during the course of our days—or nights."

Paula regarded him skeptically. "Do you mind telling us where you were last night between eight and nine?" she asked, knowing that Laurelyn was likely killed shortly after leaving the hair salon.

Eckart looked Paula directly in the eye while answering without preface, "I was at Rennie's Bar on Twenty-Second Street, having drinks with my buddy J. H. Santoro. We met there at seven and didn't leave till after midnight."

"Where can we reach this J. H. Santoro?" Gayle asked him.

"He's staying at an apartment complex on Yackley Road past Diamond Street. I have his number."

As Gayle added it to her cell phone, Paula considered digging deeper but, mindful of the arms case against him, thought better. Instead, she said evenly, "While we check out your alibi, we'll need you to come to the morgue to identify the body of Laurelyn Wong."

Chapter Eight

"J. H. Santoro is the moniker of ATF undercover agent Vinny Ortiz," Neil informed Paula after he'd invited her over to his rented house for a nightcap and she'd brazenly accepted.

"Really?" She eyed Neil as they stood in the kitchen, both holding wineglasses half-filled with red wine. Its open concept provided a nice view of the downstairs and, from the pristine looks of it, it was clear that he spent little time there socializing. She wondered if the same were true in his permanent residence. Or was it more a matter of merely having the right reason to socialize—and the right person to do so with?

"Yeah," Neil told her. "And Ortiz confirmed that he did drink the night away with Craig Eckart at Rennie's Bar—pumping the arms trafficker for information to use to take him down."

"Well, apart from that, it looks like Eckart's off the hook, insofar as the murder of Laurelyn Wong," Paula said, tasting her drink. "And ostensibly this would extend as well to all the murders perpetrated by the unsub we're referring to as the Campus Killer."

"That's a solid deduction. It feeds into the theory that, though the victims are likely being targeted by the unsub, the targeting, per se, may be more opportunity driven in a random way than the work of someone intimately acquainted with the victims." Neil sipped the wine. "This, in and of itself, would've put Eckart lower on the totem pole as the serial killer, with his girlfriend apparently the fifth victim of the unsub."

"I suppose, when you put it that way." Paula gave a little smile as Neil seemed totally in his element as an ATF special agent profiler. It made her wonder if he could ever give it up. Perhaps to become a full-time professor?

Neil grinned and said, "And what if I were to put it this way…" He lifted her chin and then kissed her solidly on the mouth. After she felt like she was floating on air, he pulled away. "What do you think?"

Paula touched her inflamed mouth and knew precisely what she was thinking. No reason to deny what she sensed they both wanted, over and beyond solving their criminal investigations. Gazing into his eyes, she responded honestly, "I'm thinking that I'd love to pick this up somewhere more comfortable."

"Such as?" he challenged her.

"Such as your bedroom." She took the bait. Why not?

"I was thinking the same thing," he uttered desirously. "Shall I lead the way?"

She took another sip of the wine, set it on the quartz island countertop and said bluntly, "Yes, please."

Neil smiled and kissed her again. "It would be my pleasure." He set down his drink and took her hand.

They headed up a central staircase to the second floor, passing by a couple of rooms down the hallway, before arriving at the primary suite. Stepping inside the spacious bedroom, they engaged in some more passionate kissing that left Paula breathless and wanting so much more. She backed away from Neil and scanned the room, taking in the midcentury modern furnishings and sash windows with Roman blinds. Her gaze landed squarely on the king-size platform bed with its fluffy pillows and navy patchwork quilt.

The thought of making love to Neil excited Paula beyond words, if the hot kisses between them were any indication. But that moment was also a realistic reawakening. Always responsible in her sexual practices, there was no reason to turn away from that now, no matter how strong the desire to have him. "Do you have protection?" she asked equably.

"Absolutely," Neil responded, as if anticipating the question. "I believe in better safe than sorry with sex too," he assured her with a straight face.

"Cool." She offered him a smile and watched as he disappeared into the bathroom and returned with the condom packet.

"Do I do this now?" Neil held it up. "Or later?"

Paula chuckled. "Uh, I think you can take your clothes off first."

He laughed. "Yeah, there is that."

She watched him set the packet atop a walnut nightstand and start to disrobe, as she did the same, feeling slightly self-conscious in the process. That went away for the most part as Paula reveled in checking out Neil's six-pack abs and the rest of his taut frame.

She hardly realized he was just as riveted on her till Neil commented, while giving Paula the once-over, "Has anyone ever told you just how gorgeous you are?"

Blushing, Paula admitted, "Not lately."

"Then I'm saying it," he declared. "You are stunning…
and perfect, all of you."

"Back at you," she assured him, gazing at him from
head to toe and in between.

They bridged the gap and resumed kissing, before
making their way to the bed, where more intimacy followed with sizzling foreplay. When she could stand it no
more, Paula cooed, "Make love to me, Neil…"

"Are you sure you're ready?"

"Oh, yes, I'm definitely ready for you," she declared.

"Then why wait a second longer," he uttered in a raspy
voice, kissing her passionately again.

After Neil put on the condom, Paula waited with bated
breath as he made his way between her legs, and she
took him in whole, meeting him two-thirds of the way
with each deep thrust into her. Their bodies pressed together and heartbeats were in sync as Paula felt the or-
gasm course through her in rapid fashion, moaning as
she quivered with delight. She clung to Neil while he
followed suit shortly thereafter, his body quaking as his
own powerful release manifested itself wildly.

When it was over, their sexual appetites satiated
through their actions and the invigorating scent of intimacy left behind, Paula rested her head on Neil's chest.
She gushed, "Wow. That was amazing!"

He laughed. "It was, wasn't it?"

She blushed. "Yeah, truly."

"Some things in life have a predictable outcome," he
suggested. "This was definitely one of them."

Paula giggled at his confidence. "Oh, you think so,
do you?"

"I saw the sparks between us early on," Neil maintained. "It was just a matter of letting the flames erupt, sizzle, or whatever."

"How poetic," she said with a chuckle but couldn't disagree, having felt the connection too practically from the moment they first laid eyes on one another. But now that the spell had been broken, where did they go from here? If anywhere?

He laughed. "You bring the poet out in me, Paula, what can I say?"

She could think of a few things, but perhaps it was best not to delve too deeply in what this could mean potentially. Realizing the time, she separated from him and said, "I have to go."

"So soon?" Neil frowned. "I was hoping we might make a night of it—continuing this carnal exploration."

"Hmm… I'd love to," she admitted, climbing off the bed, "but I need to go feed my cat."

Neil sat up. "You have a cat?"

"Yep, her name's Chloe. She gets pretty ornery when she's hungry."

"I know the feeling. Need some help?" He eyed her body devilishly.

Paula got past the self-consciousness, knowing full well he liked what he saw, and then some. "Feeding the cat?"

"Sure." He grinned sideways. "I'm pretty good with my hands."

"That you are." She laughed thoughtfully. "You're welcome to come and help feed Chloe. Or whatever," she added, leaving the door open for whatever might come next.

NEIL FOLLOWED PAULA to her penthouse condo, eager to check out her place and extend the time they got to spend together. He was admittedly still caught up in the afterglow of the mind-blowing sex they had earlier. Though confident they would click in that department, the proof was very much in the pudding, as both had measured up beyond his expectations. It made him wonder where this thing was headed. Could she see a future with him? Could he see one with her?

What Neil knew for certain was that he wanted more than one quick romp where Paula was concerned. Beyond that, he was certainly willing to keep a very open mind as to what may lay in store for them once his time as a visiting professor had run its course.

Once they reached the condominium and went inside, Paula said, waving her arms around, "Well, here we are."

"I love it," Neil told her, sizing up the condo and the furnishings that seemed a perfect fit.

"Thanks." She smiled. "Make yourself at home while I give Chloe something to eat."

"Allow me," he insisted, figuring this was a good way to score points with Paula by warming up to her cat. He spotted Chloe wandering along the baseboard as though lost. Neil enticed the cat to come his way and scooped her into his arms. He gently rubbed her head and ears. "I'm Neil," he said lightheartedly. "Let's get you fed and content for the night."

"Looks like she's warming up to you in a hurry," Paula said with amusement.

Neil grinned. "I have that effect on—" he was about to say people, or her, in particular, but changed course midsentence "—cute, furry felines."

She laughed. "I can see that."

After feeding the cat, Neil turned his attention to Paula, and vice versa, as they made their way upstairs to her bedroom and upholstered farmhouse bed for another round of sexual relations. Only this time, without the sense of urgency, Neil was able to more slowly explore Paula's beautiful face and every inch of her body, giving her the same courtesy with him, as they made love into the wee hours of the night, before sleep and sheer exhaustion overtook them.

In the morning, Neil awakened from a bad dream about a killer running amok using illegal firearms. He didn't get a look at the unsub's face, but he was certain that the nightmare was a confluence of the Campus Killer meets the gunrunner, Craig Eckart. Only the two weren't one and the same in real life, Neil knew. Meaning that both cases were still open and needed to be successfully brought to a close, with the perps taken into custody.

When turning over and expecting to find Paula, naked, hot and still bothered, instead Neil saw that her spot beneath the covers was empty. He got up, slipping on his pants that had made their way onto the wood flooring, and looked for her.

He found her downstairs in the kitchen, where his nostrils picked up the scent of cooked sausage, before Neil saw Paula fully dressed and making breakfast.

"Hey," she said, offering a smile. "Hope you like blueberry pancakes and sausage, to go with coffee?"

"Absolutely to all." He smiled back, walked up to her in his bare feet and kissed her. "But most of all, I like you." He made no bones about it.

"I like you too." She beamed. "So, let's eat and we can talk about our plans for today."

"Okay. Let me go put on the rest of my clothes and I'm all yours."

Her lashes fluttered while standing over the griddle. "We'll see about that."

Though his words may have been a metaphor, Neil felt they had a good ring to them nevertheless and he was beginning to take them quite literally. In spite of not knowing if they both had what it took to see it through, for better or worse.

IN HER OFFICE, Paula pushed past thoughts of last night's red-hot sex with Neil or whether or not she was falling in love with the ATF special agent—and instead focused on the autopsy report on her laptop on Laurelyn Wong's death. As expected, the Shays County Chief Medical Examiner Eddie Saldana ruled this as a homicide. Similar to the other homicides thought to be perpetrated by the Campus Killer, the cause of the associate professor of music education's death was asphyxia. The time of death was believed to be between 8:00 p.m. and 10:00 p.m. A towel left at the crime scene was thought to be the murder weapon.

I'm sorry you had to die this way, Paula thought, knowing that Laurelyn Wong, like the other victims, had plans for her life. Now these had been squelched permanently by a cold-blooded killer who decided their lives were not worth living.

But who was the unsub? With Laurelyn's lover, Craig Eckart, ruled out, it brought Paula back to Neil's student, Roger Woodward. He had alibis for the murders of two of his professors, Debra Newton and Odette Furillo. But Paula had yet to check out his alibi for Professor Wong's murder. Was he enrolled in Laurelyn Wong's music class?

Pulling up Woodward's class schedule, Paula did not see him as a student of Laurelyn's. She checked the last semester and got the same result. Similarly, there was no information that directly linked the honors student to professors Harmeet Fernández or Kathy Payne. But did that mean he was innocent? Or a clever serial killer, above and beyond an obviously bright senior?

AT THE SCHOOL OF CRIMINAL JUSTICE, Neil sat in the conference room with the other faculty and two teaching assistants, Desmond Isaac and Rachelle Kenui. Director Stafford Geeson, the former police chief of Mackinac Island, Michigan, had convened the hastily arranged meeting to talk about the pipe bombs discovered in the building yesterday.

Geeson, who was fifty-five and thickly built, with slicked-back gray hair and a receding hairline, stood in front of the room and shifted his blue eyes as he said earnestly, "I'm sure everyone here knows about the bomb incident that took place on the ground floor of Horton Hall. Though the Regional Special Response Team was able to locate the pipe bombs and deactivate them before they could explode, it's still troubling that this happened on campus—and in this building, in particular." His chin sagged. "As of now, the perpetrator or perpetrators remain at large. Till apprehended, I'm asking everyone who works for the School of Criminal Justice to be extra diligent in looking out for anyone acting suspicious. The directors of the other departments in this building are telling staff the same thing. And if you know anyone who might have a beef against someone in Horton Hall or the university itself, don't hesitate to bring this to my attention or the authorities."

Geeson took a breath and, eyeing Neil, said, "As our resident criminal profiler, Professor Ramirez, I'm hoping you can maybe shed some light on the pipe bomber and what's behind this terroristic attack on the campus."

Neil said evenly, "Sure, I can shed a bit of light on the subject." He had anticipated he might be called upon in this manner. Standing, he walked to the front of the room, got a pat on the shoulder from the director, and then Neil got right to it, saying thoughtfully, "Well, without being privy to the specifics about the current case, my general view on bomber unsubs is that they tend to be narcissists who choose to use fear tactics such as a bomb threat to get attention and/or cause death and destruction as a matter of retaliation for perceived wrongs against them. Or to make a statement of one type or another.

"Though they are often loners," he explained, "and obviously antisocial, some are paranoid schizophrenics, while others are mentally sound but still willing to involve themselves in abnormal behavior for reasons aforementioned. We'll have to see which way the pendulum swings in this instance."

Desmond asked, "So, are we talking about a student or ex-student bomber with a grudge against the school or a professor?"

Neil peered at him. "Is there something you want to confess to us, Isaac?" he asked the TA lightheartedly.

"Not that I can think of," Desmond said with a chuckle.

"Just checking." Neil flashed a crooked grin. "As for whether or not the unsub is a current or former student, that's a distinct possibility. But—" he felt it needed to be emphasized "—the perp could also be an employee or ex-worker at the university. As well as someone who has no connection at all, but found the campus location attractive and had the means to both use the library to announce the bomb threat and deliver the pipe bombs, while managing to get away."

"Sounds very much like the Campus Killer," Rachelle Kenui remarked. The twentysomething TA was thin, green-eyed and had short wheat-blond hair in a mullet cut. "Could they be one and the same?"

"Anything's possible," Neil stated. "Generally speaking, though, unless we're talking about a serial bomber, heaven forbid, the profiles of a single incident bomber and serial killer do not usually measure up. As for the school bomber, hopefully we'll get a better idea of who—and what—we're looking for once forensics has examined the pipe bombs for DNA, prints, etc."

After a little more insight into the bombing incident, the meeting broke up and Neil headed to his office to prepare for his next class. Even with the current uneasiness on campus, given the unusual criminal activity of late, he wanted to keep the classes as normal as possible for his students, in spite of Neil knowing that this would be next to impossible. As long as a serial killer and pipe bomber remained on the loose.

Chapter Nine

Paula walked down the fifth-floor corridor in the Acklin Residence Hall on Wells Lane. Along the way, she passed a group of giggling female students, before reaching Room 557. The door was open, and Paula could see a slender young woman with multicolored long hair, standing while looking at her cell phone. A knock got her attention. "Are you Adriana Tilly?"

"Yes, I'm Adriana." She put the phone in the back pocket of her jeans.

Paula stepped inside the cluttered two-person room and showed her identification. "Detective Lynley. I'm investigating the murder of Honors College Associate Professor Odette Furillo. Mind if I ask you a few questions…?"

Adriana arched a thin brow worriedly. "You think I had something to do with that?"

"I'm sure you didn't," Paula responded, giving her the benefit of the doubt. "A name that's come up in the investigation is of one of Professor Furillo's students—Roger Woodward. Do you know him?" she asked for effect.

Her blue eyes grew wide. "Yes. Roger's my boyfriend."

"He says that he was with you the night Professor Furillo was killed," Paula said, giving her the date and time frame. "I need you to verify his alibi."

Adriana wasted little time doing just that. "Yes, Roger was with me the entire night," she confirmed unabashedly.

Paula gave her a direct look. "You're sure about that?"

"Yes." She paused before adding, "Roger would never kill anyone. Certainly not one of his professors."

Maybe you don't know your boyfriend as well as you think, Paula thought, aware that denial was often the order of the day when someone you were close to was suspected of murder. "Had to ask as part of my job," she told her. While at it, for the record, Paula thought to ask if Woodward was with her when Professor Laurelyn Wong was killed. Adriana claimed calmly that he was.

With no real reason to dispute this, Paula went with that and saw herself out. It appeared as if Neil's student, Roger Woodward, was not their Campus Killer. Which meant that the hunt to unmask and apprehend the unsub was still on.

At 4:00 p.m., Neil pulled his car up behind Agent Vinny Ortiz's Jeep Wagoneer on Quail Lane in Rendall Creek Park. Ortiz, aka J. H. Santoro as his undercover handle, had requested the meeting to discuss the latest developments in the arms trafficking investigation. For his part, Neil was curious as to whether the murder of suspected gunrunner Craig Eckart's girlfriend, Laurelyn Wong, had changed the dynamics of the case any.

Ortiz exited the Jeep and made his way to the passenger side of Neil's Chevy Suburban, where Ortiz muttered, "Thanks for meeting with me on short notice."

Neil regarded him. "What's up?"

"Not sure," the undercover agent said flatly. "With the death of Eckart's girlfriend, Laurelyn, at the hands purportedly of a serial killer, it's kind of freaking the man out."

"How so?" Neil hesitated to ask.

"Well, apparently Eckart feels it's bad karma that someone he had a thing for has been murdered. He's wondering if it's trying to tell him something."

"Such as?"

"If he has an X on his own back," Ortiz said bluntly. "Though Eckart was glad we happened to be hanging out at a bar together the night she was killed, he believes Laurelyn's death is a sign that he needs to put his plans for arms trafficking into a higher gear—so that he can get rich and maybe get out of the business."

"That so?" Neil didn't see that happening of his own free will, karma or not. For most traders of contraband small arms and ammo—especially when operating on the dark web—the money they could make and perceived lower risk of detection made the illicit activities almost addictive. He doubted it was something Craig Eckart could easily walk away from, even though someone had murdered his girlfriend. Neil gazed at the ATF agent. "What do you think?"

Ortiz shrugged. "I don't see him calling it quits. He's got too nice of an operation going. Or so he thinks. But I do believe that Eckart is even more suspicious that he's being set up. Meaning, I have to go even deeper undercover to protect myself, without stepping over the line."

"Do what you need to do," Neil advised him. "Be smart about it. We can get you help whenever you need it."

"I'll keep that in mind." Ortiz scratched his beard-stache. "I think things are about to go down. When it happens, I'll be sure to get the word out so we can nail this bastard. Hopefully, before any more illegal weapons can change hands, in this country or abroad."

"The team will be ready to pounce," Neil assured, wanting this to be over almost as much as Ortiz did.

Ortiz tilted his face with curiosity. "So, with Laurelyn yet another victim, are you any closer to getting the jump on the Campus Killer?"

Neil furrowed his forehead. "I'd like to think we're closing in on the unsub with each and every hour," he responded, his voice steady and thoughtful. "But that's not exactly the same as knowing who we're dealing with and having him locked up behind bars, is it?"

"No, it isn't." Ortiz sighed. "You'll get the perp. He can't go on killing professors forever and not have to face the music for his crimes."

"I'm thinking the same thing." Neil squirmed. "Not much consolation, though, for those who fall prey to the unsub." This told him that the task force needed to step up even more than they already were, if this meant sparing the lives of other professors that could come within the unsub's viewfinder.

"Talk to you soon," Ortiz said succinctly.

Neil nodded. "Yeah."

After Ortiz drove off, Neil followed suit and once again found himself weighing his options on what to do with the rest of his life beyond his current caseload. Was he truly cut out for being a full-time educator? Or was being an ATF special agent and behavioral profiler too much in his blood to ever truly want to walk away from?

Then there was Paula. She had come into his life practically out of the blue. And just at a time when he wasn't
sure he would ever again click with a woman who could
earn his trust. She had already passed both tests with
flying colors. But would he be enough to check all the
boxes she had for a workable relationship, after falling
short in her marriage to another man who made his living in federal law enforcement?

Neil knew that whatever decisions he made could well
rest on how he fared on Paula's litmus test or desire to
carry on with what they had started.

ON WEDNESDAY AFTERNOON, the latest task force briefing
took place at the Rendall Cove Police Department. Gayle
stood alongside Paula at the podium in the conference
room, knowing that all eyes were on them as they had
to give the highlights and lowlights of the investigation
now that yet another victim had been added to the list
of those targeted by the Campus Killer. This was starting to get old in a hurry, Gayle felt, sure that Paula concurred. But this was where they were and they had to
put on their best faces in meeting the challenge head-on.

Holding the stylus pen, Gayle turned to the large monitor and brought up the image of the latest victim to die at
the hands of an unsub. "Two nights ago, Laurelyn Wong,
a thirty-two-year-old music professor, was murdered in
her vehicle, after having her hair done at a salon on Fulmore Street," Gayle reported. "According to the autopsy
report, Professor Wong's death was due to asphyxia, with
the murder weapon being a cotton towel. It was the same
cause of death attributed to four other female professors
at Addison University. Though the investigation is well

underway and we're looking at each and every angle here, as of now, the killer remains at large..."

Gayle swallowed as she looked at the man in charge of the Detective Bureau, Criminal Investigations Sergeant Anderson Klimack. At fifty-five and solid in build beneath his uniform, with short, tapered brown-gray hair parted to the side and blue eyes, he was bucking to become lieutenant. She was sure that putting this case behind the bureau would help him make his case for the promotion.

Averting his stare, while feeling the pressure, Gayle made a few more comments, before turning it over to Paula, who gave her a supportive little smile and then said in a serious tone, "Losing another professor to a senseless murder is something none of us wanted to hear. Much less have to investigate. But a cold and calculating serial killer has reared his ugly head again in targeting the popular music professor Laurelyn Wong. In the process, the unsub has put us on notice that he has no intention of ending the killing of professors off and on campus—not till we stop him."

After going over the victims again, locations of the murders and efforts to gather forensic evidence and surveillance video on the latest homicide as with the earlier deaths, Gayle and Paula took turns laying out the investigative efforts. Neither sought to sugarcoat the frustrations within the task force in its inability to solve the case as yet. But both insisted that this made them even more determined to do just that—whatever it took.

Davenport and another investigator from the Detective Bureau, Larry Coolidge, a tall and bald-headed five-year veteran of the PD, provided additional updates; then

Neil pitched in with observations, while doing his best to try and put the Campus Killer case into proper perspective by stating coolly, "Undoubtedly, losing five women in the prime of their lives to a serial killer is almost too much to bear for all of us. But, just to be clear, the number of victims thus far pales to those killed by such serial monsters as Samuel Little, who murdered at least sixty women over several decades, Gary Ridgway, convicted of forty-nine murders, Juan Corona, found guilty of killing twenty-five. Even the infamous female serial killer, Belle Gunness, claimed at least fourteen victims. Or, in other words, we have time to stop the perp long before he can reach these goals as a serial killer."

To Gayle—and she read as much in Paula's expression— this was something to keep in mind as further motivation to prevent the unsub from joining the ranks of these killers in their bloodthirsty appetite for murder.

THAT NIGHT, Paula slept in Neil's bed, where the two recreated the first time they made love. Only this occasion was more thorough, demanding, fervent and, yes, all-consuming. Neither seemed to want it to end. At least this was how Paula read the passion. Could she have mistaken Neil's body language for anything other than being just as intoxicated by the experience?

When they were totally spent and gratified, she laid in his arms, with neither saying a word. For her part, Paula hesitated sharing her thoughts for fear of having her heart broken. Telling someone you were starting to fall in love with them could backfire, she believed. Especially if it was not reciprocated by a person who likely wouldn't be around much longer. She wondered if there was any wiggle room in the special agent's future plans. Or were they set in stone, and he had no desire to start a relationship he couldn't finish?

IN THE MORNING, they got up early for a run in the park. Had it been up to Neil, he would have let Paula get more sleep and gone it alone. Between the passionate love-making and restlessness from the stresses associated with tracking a serial killer, neither had gotten much shut-eye. But she had been insistent upon joining him, having kept jogging clothes in her car for that purpose.

If the truth be told, Neil welcomed her company, as Paula was growing on him in ways that he could never have anticipated fully upon coming to Rendall Cove. Last night only reinforced that. Having someone to open his heart to again excited him. He could tell that the feeling was mutual. But there was still the matter of what it all meant for the future. And if their relationship had what it took to survive the criminal investigations that brought them together.

The run was mostly silent, aside from the chirping sounds of black-capped chickadees in the woods. After taking turns racing ahead of the other, Neil broke the ice by asking perceptively, "What's on your mind?"

Paula faced him and said point-blank, "You…and wondering where this—" she pointed her finger at him and then herself "—is going. Or do you even know?"

He took a breath. "I'm wondering the same thing," he admitted, following with, "Honestly, I haven't a clue."

"That's helpful," she said sarcastically.

"Not sure what you expect me to say." He stiffened. "I care for you, Paula. I'm sure you know that. I think that we have something here." Another pause came. "I'm just not sure how things will play out once my time at the university is up. Are you?" If she had a concrete plan for them, he was certainly ready to listen.

Paula sucked in a deep breath. "No, not really," she confessed.

"So why don't we just go with the flow and see how things turn out?" Neil put forth. He hoped he wasn't backing her into a corner so she wanted to end things between them prematurely.

"All right." She favored him with a convivial smile. "We'll do that."

"Good." *That tells me she wants this to work as much as I do*, he told himself. This gave Neil hope that they were truly on the same wavelength. Even if the future was still very much up in the air. But at least it had given them a sense of direction that neither could turn away from.

WHEN THEY ARRIVED back at his house, Paula was still pondering the prospects for making a life with Neil. Or not. With much dependent upon who would be willing to sacrifice the most in making this work between them. Selfishly, she would love to see him stay in Rendall Cove as a professor. But was that even feasible? Could she handle giving up her job, if it came right down to it, in the name of love? Or would she be falling into an old pattern with predictable results?

Her reverie was broken while they were in the kitchen making breakfast—French toast, orange juice and coffee—when both their cell phones rang at the same time. Paula grabbed hers first and saw that the caller was Mike Davenport. "Hey," she answered.

"If you're by the television, you might want to put on the news to see what's about to break."

As she was hanging up with Davenport, she saw that Neil had been told the same thing, as he had already stepped inside the living room and was holding the TV remote, turning the set on. Joining him, Paula watched the flat-screen LCD television as an attractive red-haired female news anchor was saying animatedly, "An arrest has been made in connection with the pipe bombs found two days ago at Horton Hall on the campus of Addison University." An image of a dark-haired, grim-faced young man appeared on the screen. "According to sources, taken into custody was Harold Fujisawa—a twenty-two-year-old former student at the university. The global history major, who was reportedly expelled from school last year because of unspecified threats made, was arrested without incident outside a café on Long Street in Shays County."

Neil cut the TV off and, with his brow furrowed, uttered, "Looks like we've nipped one headache in the bud."

"Hope so." Paula wrinkled her nose thoughtfully. The arrest of the pipe bomb suspect was certainly a relief. "The university doesn't need a disgruntled ex-student resorting to terrorism to settle a score."

"Tell me about it." Neil met her eyes. "Nor does it need a serial killer run amok. But that will be dealt with too."

She nodded agreeably. "Not soon enough."

"I'm with you." He put his hands on her shoulders, pulling them closer. "In more ways than one."

"Same here," she promised him, resolving not to look

too far ahead while still trying to sort out feelings and happenings between them in present terms.

When Neil dipped his head and kissed her, Paula returned the kiss in full, enjoying the firmness of his mouth upon hers and the overall way it made her feel.

Minutes later, they returned to the kitchen and the French toast, ate the breakfast and talked about the crimes being investigated, while avoiding discussing things best left off the table for the time being.

Chapter Ten

That morning, Neil attended a Regional Special Response Team briefing in a Shays County Sheriff's Department conference room. The subject matter was the pipe bomb terrorist attack on the Addison University campus. Neil was all ears in wanting to know just how they identified and took down the suspect. Just as important was whether or not the perp could have been involved in the suffocation murders of female professors.

RSRT Lieutenant Corey Chamberlain was at the podium, giving the update. "As you know by now, at approximately seven twenty-nine a.m. today, we made an arrest in relation to the pipe bombs planted at the university. The suspect is Harold Fujisawa, who was kicked out of the school at the junior level last fall, due to making threats against faculty in the College of Social Science, where he was enrolled, after he was caught cheating on exams. Though there were no formal charges filed, Fujisawa, twenty-two, had been on our radar ever since.

"We were able to link him to the computer used at the school library to post bomb threats on social media through forensic analysis and surveillance video," Chamberlain said. "Once identified, we located the suspect—who was apparently living on the streets these days—at the Creekside Café. We waited for him to emerge before placing Harold Fujisawa under arrest. He made a full confession, blaming his actions on an addiction to the so-called zombie drug, Xylazine. Mr. Fujisawa is being charged with a number of federal offenses related to the manufacturing and possession of an explosive device, planting two pipe bombs on university property and more…" The lieutenant took a breath. "As of now, we believe the suspect acted alone."

Neil was confident that Harold Fujisawa would no longer pose a threat to Addison University or the city at large. But it still begged another important question that needed to be answered. "What can you tell us about the suspect's DNA and prints in relation to any other crimes?" Neil asked interestedly.

Chamberlain ran a hand across his face and responded, "We collected a sample of Fujisawa's DNA, along with fingerprinting him. The DNA was put into CODIS to check for a match. Unfortunately, it came back negative."

Or, in other words, Fujisawa's DNA was not a match for the unknown DNA profile taken from beneath the nails of a victim of the Campus Killer, Neil told himself, which corresponded with his feelings that the serial killer and pipe bomber were likely two different perpetrators. "And the prints?"

Chamberlain frowned perceptively. "The suspect doesn't have a criminal history to work with. So, no fingerprints on file and verified as such through the Michigan Automated Fingerprint Identification System."

Which, Neil knew, corresponded with the FBI and Homeland Security AFIS. Meaning that Harold Fujisawa almost certainly wasn't at the crime scenes of the

murdered professors, with no match to any of the finger
and palm prints collected and entered into the databases.

As such, his attention as a profiler had to be refo-
cused on an unsub in the search for the Campus Killer.
Neil thought about Paula, who had left his rented house
shortly after breakfast. He believed they had turned the
corner somewhat in their relationship, even if neither
of them knew precisely what road they were headed
down. Or how long it might take to get there. But at this
point, he would take any positive development in terms
of building something together, which he felt ready for
at this point. He could only hope she would not let her
own past romance drama stand in the way of what they
could potentially have.

PAULA STOOD ON the deck, observing Canada geese hud-
dled together by the creek, as she called her former sister-
in-law, Madison. They had stayed in touch as real friends,
in spite of Paula's divorce from her brother, Scott.

When Madison came onto the small screen, her bold
turquoise eyes lit up, surrounded by an attractive face
and long blond hair worn in a shaggy wolf cut with curly
bangs. "Hey, there," she said sweetly.

"Hey." Paula grinned, noting that Madison was in
uniform as a full-time law enforcement ranger in the
Blue Ridge Mountains of North Carolina. She had recently gotten married to a National Park Service Investigative Services Branch special agent. "How's life
treating you these days in the ranger's world?"

"Good. Rarely a dull moment on and off the Blue
Ridge Parkway," Madison told her, referencing the 469-
mile National Scenic Byway that meandered through

North Carolina and Virginia. "Keeps me on my toes. What's up with you?"

"Well, besides investigating a serial killer on campus and surviving a bomb threat in one piece—" Paula pretended like they were merely run-of-the-mill occurrences "—I've met someone," she ventured forth. She felt comfortable sharing this with her, knowing Madison had encouraged her to move on past Scott.

"As if a serial killer and bomber aren't enough to deal with, right?" Madison made a face. "We'll get back to that. So, who have you met and it's about time…?"

"His name is Neil Ramirez," Paula told her. "Neil's an ATF special agent who's currently a visiting professor at the university."

"Hmm…" Madison widened her eyes with curiosity. "Interesting. Tell me more."

Paula did just that, while not getting carried away in her fondness for the man. Or what may or may not be in store for them. Only that they got along well and liked one another. "We'll see how it goes," she finished with, resisting the urge to admit she hoped it could go as far as possible between two people attracted to one another.

"I'm definitely pulling for you," Madison promised. "You deserve to be happy. We all do."

"Thanks, Madison." Paula knew she was referring to her ex as well and had no problem with that, wishing him the happiness that had eluded them over the long term. She told Madison a bit more about her current investigation before hanging up.

After setting out food for Chloe, Paula headed off to work.

IN THE AFTERNOON, Neil had the pleasure of having not one, but two teaching assistants in Desmond Isaac and Rachelle Kenui on hand to pass out the essay exams in the Auditorium on Slane Drive, where Neil taught a class in criminology to a captive audience of students. He was optimistic that they would be able to keep their eyes on the ball, as it were, even in the midst of some of the unsettling events happening on campus of late.

Handing Desmond and Rachelle a batch of the exams, Neil joked, "Think you two can handle this very tough assignment and earn your stripes?"

Rachelle giggled. "Can't speak for Desmond here, but I believe I'm more than up to the task."

Desmond gave a little laugh. "It's going to be challenging, I admit," he quipped, "but I'll just have to push myself harder and not quit before I get started."

Neil chuckled. "Figured I could count on you both." He grabbed more of the exams from his briefcase. "So, let's do this before my class thinks they'll get lucky and get a free pass here, or a delayed exam. Not happening."

"Not on our watch," Rachelle agreed, flashing her teeth.

Desmond looked at her and said, "As Prof Ramirez said, let's get this over with, and we can have fun watching them sweat it out while seeing if they've learned anything."

"They better have," she voiced in earnest.

Neil eyed the two TAs as they headed toward the students seated throughout the lecture hall. He suspected that Rachelle and Desmond may have started dating. Whether this meant they had a future together was anyone's guess. Neil was more concerned about his own relationship with

Paula and if the love he was feeling for her was the real deal. If so, he didn't want to blow it with her. But he did have his career to think about too. As did she as a campus detective sergeant. Was there enough room in their lives for each other when all was said and done?

PAULA WAS IN her office going over notes on the Campus Killer case when the Addison University alert came in, reporting a suspected armed robbery near the Communication Arts and Sciences Building on Rafton Street. The suspect was described by the female victim as a tall, slender and blue-eyed female in her early twenties, wearing dark clothes and a hoodie that was still able to expose curly crimson hair beneath. Patrol officers had been dispatched to the location, with the unsub having fled the scene and still at large.

Hmm, that's not too far from here, Paula thought, getting up from her chair. Maybe she could help nail the culprit, even if it was a distraction from her current investigation. She checked the SIG Sauer P365 semiautomatic pistol tucked in her concealment holster and then was out the door.

No sooner had she left the building and was about to hop into her car, when Paula spotted someone who resembled the unsub running north down the sidewalk. Trailing her, Paula narrowed the distance, while noting that the suspect appeared to be holding a pocketknife. *No match for a loaded gun*, Paula told herself.

Removing the semiautomatic pistol, she wasted no time barking orders to the suspect. "Stop! Drop the weapon!"

The young woman stopped on a dime and rounded

on her. "This isn't what you think," she expressed, with the hood still covering her head.

"I've heard that line too many times," Paula said sardonically. "I'm Detective Lynley, campus police department. Drop the weapon—please—so I don't have to shoot you."

"Okay, I give up." She placed the knife on the sidewalk and pulled the hood down, revealing a cropped red pixie around a pretty heart-shaped face, and then raised her hands.

"Keep them raised!" While keeping the gun aimed, Paula approached her carefully and ordered, "Turn around." The suspect obeyed and Paula removed chained handcuffs from a nylon handcuff holster attached to her waistband on the back side and, twisting the suspect's arms around, quickly cuffed her. "So, what's your name?"

"Nikki Simone."

Paula faced her. "Are you a student here?"

"Yeah. I'm a senior."

And you want to destroy your life this close to graduating, Paula mused sadly. "Nikki, you're under arrest for a suspected armed robbery," she told her flatly.

"I never robbed her," Nikki snapped. "I only took what was rightly mine—the engagement ring she got from my ex-boyfriend, Lester Siegel. He gave it to me, then stole it from me, once I ended things after I caught him cheating on me with her."

Paula lifted a brow to the tale that seemed too incredible to be untrue. "You have the ring on you?"

"Yeah, in my pocket." Her eyes watered. "I just wanted it to remember him from when things were good, you know?"

"I sympathize with you," Paula had to admit. "Unfortunately, you went about getting back your property the wrong way and will now need to sort it out through the criminal justice system. If you're lucky, your ex won't press charges and you can chalk this—and him—up to a bad experience."

As a squad car approached, Paula reluctantly turned the suspect over to the two fresh-faced officers, while explaining the situation as the suspect told it to her, leaving it for them to decide if they wanted to let her go.

She texted Neil to see if he wanted to grab a coffee. He quickly responded, asking her to meet him at the Auditorium, where he had a class. Agreeing, Paula headed for her car, still wondering how they might make things work once Neil's stint as a visiting professor was over. Did any long-distance, relatively speaking, relationships ever work over the long term? Or might they find an acceptable way to bridge the gap?

After parking, Paula went inside the Auditorium and had just arrived at the lecture hall as the students were filing out. She went inside and saw Neil conversing near the front with a twentysomething male and female.

Neil looked up and grinned when he saw Paula and said, "Hey."

"Hi," she responded.

"These are my teaching assistants, Desmond Isaac and Rachelle Kenui." Neil introduced them. "Detective Paula Lynley."

"Hey," the two TAs said in unison, smiling.

"Hey." Paula smiled back at them.

"They make my job a whole lot easier," Neil claimed.

"I'm sure they do." Paula went along with this.

"I think it's more the other way around," Desmond said. "Prof Ramirez is easy to work with."

"True." Rachelle beamed and regarded Desmond. "We should go."

"Yeah." He placed a hand on the small of her back. "Let's get out of here." He eyed Neil. "We'll have the graded essays to you tomorrow afternoon."

Neil nodded. "Good."

"Later," he told Neil and glanced smilingly at Paula and back to Rachelle.

After they left, Paula asked Neil, "Are you ready?"

"Yeah. Let me just get my briefcase."

They walked in silence the short distance to the Union Building food court, where both ordered lattes and took a seat.

"Got a briefing on the bombing at Horton Hall," Neil remarked, sipping the coffee. "Looks as though the suspect, Harold Fujisawa, had a beef against the College of Social Science faculty after being expelled. This was his misguided attempt at payback, using the excuse of being high on Xylazine to justify his actions."

"Excuses, excuses." Paula rolled her eyes and shook her head. "When will they ever learn?"

"Not soon enough for too many." Neil sat back. "Though Fujisawa's going down for various terrorism charges, he's not the Campus Killer unsub. His DNA and prints didn't match those found at any of the crime scenes of the serial murders."

Paula tasted the latte and said, "Not too surprised to hear that." She noted that Neil had already, more or less, believed that the unsub bomber didn't fit the profile of the Campus Killer and vice versa. "Would've been nice though if the two perps were one and the same and we could have wrapped up our case in one fell swoop." She shrugged. "Oh, well…"

"That's the way it goes," Neil said, taking it in stride. "There are many dangerous individuals out there waiting to do bad things that we have to clean up, one way or the other."

"You're right. Can't exactly read their minds ahead of time, can we?"

He tilted his head to the left side. "If only."

Paula thought about her latest crime incident. "I just caught an armed robbery suspect," she told him.

"Really?" Neil gazed at her. "I saw the campus alert through the emergency notification system on my cell phone."

"Yeah. Only it wasn't exactly what I expected." She drank the coffee, then recounted the unbelievable circumstances that apparently led up to the armed robbery.

Neil laughed. "Talk about getting on one's bad side, not once, but twice…"

Paula thought of the irony, knowing that Neil had been the victim of a cheating girlfriend. Only he had handled it much differently—thank goodness. "I guess when it comes to having one's heart broken, and having the audacity to take back the ring for good measure, people can lose their minds."

"Unfortunately, that's true," he concurred thoughtfully. "For some of us, we simply move on from infidelity and try not to look back."

She favored him with a thin, pensive smile. "I think that's the best way to go."

"Me too." He grinned at her, and Paula felt a tingle

from its effect on her and the firm belief that he was better off having gotten past a failed relationship. As had she. While positioning themselves to learn from it in forging new paths toward happiness.

When her cell phone rang, Paula paused those thoughts and lifted it off the table. She saw that the caller was Davenport and answered, "Hey." She listened to the detective and said tersely in response, "All right."

Neil fixed her intuitively. "What?"

Paula's chin jutted as she responded bleakly, "A female professor has been reported missing."

Chapter Eleven

Charlotte Guthrie, a forty-one-year-old associate professor of fisheries management in the Department of Fisheries and Wildlife at the College of Agriculture and Natural Resources, was last seen late yesterday afternoon. The avid runner and widow loved to jog on campus and had apparently gone for a run after finishing her last class of the day at 4:00 p.m. With her blue Tesla Model 3 located in the employee parking lot, and no signs of a break-in or other criminal activity, a search for the missing professor had begun on the campus grounds.

"I don't like the looks of this," Paula voiced as a gut feeling told her that the professor's disappearance would not end well. From all accounts, Charlotte Guthrie was a responsible and careful person and not prone to disappearing like a magician in a staged performance without explanation. No, Paula sensed that her mysterious absence was far more sinister in light of the murdered female professors at the university, two of which occurred on campus. Charlotte's faculty photograph—she was white, attractive and hazel-eyed with shoulder-length blond hair, parted to the side—had been posted on the school newspaper site and popular social media sites for Addison University students online.

"Neither do I," Neil said, as they joined in the search, walking through dense shrubbery near the Pencock Building, where the college was located and the professor had completed her last class. "There is the possibility that she was kidnapped by someone and could still be alive."

"Yes, that's a possibility," Paula allowed. Realistically, she wasn't very enthusiastic that this was an abduction that Professor Guthrie would be able to walk away from. The more likely scenario was that she had run into harm's way from which there would be no escape for her. Still, why put the cart ahead of the horse? Stranger things had happened. Maybe, just maybe, the professor hadn't been targeted by the Campus Killer. Or even someone else.

As a runner herself, who had occasionally run off course and could have potentially gotten hurt with a stumble here or there, Paula didn't discount altogether the possibility that Charlotte had injured herself during the run and, against the odds, been unable to call for help. Or hadn't been discovered by someone.

If that's the case, hopefully, we can find you in time, Paula told herself, as she moved alongside Neil, with Davenport, Gayle and others ahead and behind them, in what had quickly become a desperate search for the missing associate professor—with her very life possibly hanging in the balance. If she was alive at all.

As they moved along the banks of the Cedar River, Paula heard Davenport yell, with a disturbing catch to his voice, "I think we may have found her—"

Paula raced ahead with Neil, until they came upon an area with a large group of mallard ducks congregating by the river. Thick fauna lined the winding riverbank. In it, Paula spotted what was undeniably a thin and pale arm. She cringed when, upon closer inspection, it became clear that it was the arm of an adult female, who lay face down in the dirt.

"IT'S PROFESSOR GUTHRIE!" A petite female student, with a face-framing layered brunette bob and wearing pink square glasses, shrieked from outside the perimeter of the cordoned-off crime scene as the Shays County Chief Medical Examiner Eddie Saldana turned the decedent's body over.

Neil had already reached that conclusion, along with Paula, Gayle and Davenport, based on the physical description of the missing professor, along with her attire of an orange striped V-neck T-shirt, black track pants and white running sneakers. Beyond that, he could see that her blond hair was matted around a dirt-smudged face. Though there was no murder weapon or signs of trauma, with the generally good shape that the professor appeared to be in as a runner, there was little doubt in Neil's mind that she was the victim of foul play. He guessed that, based upon the initial positioning of the body, she had likely been caught from behind and forced down to the dirt before being able to adequately react.

Saldana was of the same mind and said, his brow furrowed, "The decedent appears to have been suffocated by someone pressing her face down into the soft dirt till she could breathe no more. I would estimate the time of death to be somewhere between four p.m. and six p.m. the prior day."

"So, we're looking at a homicide, to be sure?" Paula threw out, her expression exaggerated.

"That would be my preliminary conclusion," the chief medical examiner responded levelly, flexing the nitrile gloves he wore.

Gayle pursed her lips. "She was obviously targeted by our serial killer—"

Saldana's chin sagged. "I would assume this to be the work of the so-called Campus Killer, based on the similarities to the recent murders of Addison University female professors. But that will need further investigation from us all, I think."

"It's pretty clear to me that this is the work of our serial killer," Davenport said bluntly. "The MO is there, along with the calling card, if you will. In this case, it's the victim herself, whose death was by asphyxia, I'm sure you'll confirm, Dr. Saldana."

"Can't argue with you there, Detective," he concurred. Then, almost as an afterthought, Saldana lifted one of Charlotte Guthrie's discolored hands, studying it like an archeologist might a rare artifact. "Looks like there might be blood beneath at least two of the fingernails."

"Which likely belongs to her attacker," Neil ascertained.

"Seems a reasonable conclusion, unless proven otherwise," Saldana said, standing and removing his gloves. "We'll get her to the morgue and have the autopsy completed by ten a.m. tomorrow."

Paula angled her face and said with a sigh, "I look forward to your report, even if the results are predictable, more or less."

Davenport added humorlessly, "Hate to say it, Doc,

but she's right. The autopsy reports are beginning to sound all too familiar these days—not too surprisingly."

Saldana refused to take the bait. "Let's just wait and see," he said in a toneless voice.

Neil considered the probability that the DNA would be a match for the forensic unknown profile collected from beneath the nails of Professor Odette Furillo. Which would therefore tie the two homicides to one unsub, plausibly connecting them to the other murders attributed to a single killer.

After the victim's body was removed, crime scene technicians went about their duties searching for evidence, and investigators were dispatched to interview witnesses and persons who knew Charlotte Guthrie, as well as access surveillance videos on campus that might reveal the unsub's identity or other useful information. Neil watched as Paula directed things like a maestro. He knew that she was in her element as a university detective sergeant and seemed as though her feet were planted firmly on the ground insofar as having made a solid career on the college campus.

Unlike him, who was there on a short-term contract. Would she ever be comfortable relocating to Grand Rapids—hours away—where they could be closer? Or would it be unfair to ask her to upend her life again, after having moved from Kentucky to Rendall Cove? Could they give it a go even if they were living their lives hundreds of miles apart?

Or would one or the other need to be totally unselfish in breaking from comfort level and any necessary sacrifices in the name of finding love and all the happiness that came with it?

THE CAMPUS KILLER watched gleefully as bystanders and law enforcement wandered around in seemingly a state of shock near the banks of the Cedar River, where the latest body had been found as intended. Professor Charlotte Guthrie had made it painfully easy for him to pick up her routine, play nice and then, once she let her guard down, strike with total efficiency and satisfaction.

As she staggered from the blow he'd landed to her head from behind, it didn't take much to assist her into falling flat on her face onto the dirt. He pounced upon her like a leopard and held her head down, ignoring the indecipherable sounds that somehow managed to escape her mouth. They didn't last long before there was total silence, save for the quacking mallards hanging out lazily along the river's outer banks and a flock of cedar waxwings occupying sprawling eastern red cedar trees that bordered it.

His work was done, as he'd added the good-looking associate professor to his list of killings and had once again gotten away with it. But even he didn't believe that would be a given every time. The authorities weren't that naive. Sooner or later, they might figure things out. Or maybe they never would and this might never end. Either way, he needed to hedge his bets, so he didn't wind up going down—and never getting up again.

He regarded Detectives Paula Lynley and Gayle Yamasaki. They were conversing almost conspiratorially. He could only imagine what they were talking about. Most likely him. Wouldn't they love to get their hands on him. If the detectives played their cards right, he just might give them their wish.

Only it would be on his terms. Not theirs. And with

him having the advantage of being invisible in clear view, he was totally in the driver's seat and would have no problem running them down, metaphorically speaking. In reality, should this come to pass, he'd rather they met the same fate as the other victims of the Campus Killer.

Only time would tell.

He looked grim-faced while playing his part to mourn the loss of the professor as another educator fell victim to a murderer on the loose who no one could seem to lay a finger on.

AFTER WORK, Paula met up with Gayle at the Rendall Cove Gym on Newberry Drive. Paula loved going to the gym as a way to decompress and stay fit at the same time. She had a like mind in her fellow police detective and wasn't afraid to take advantage of that. They both had on their workout clothes as they moved their arms and legs on the side-by-side elliptical exercise machines.

"It's so annoying," Gayle complained, "having this jerk picking off professors like flies and right under our noses."

"I know, right?" Paula didn't disagree with her in the slightest. How could she when they were singing out of the same book of hymns. Only there was nothing lyrical about a serial killer targeting women working in higher education. Nor was there any reason to believe he planned to stop the killing any time soon. Not as long as he stayed seemingly a few steps ahead of their efforts to capture him. "The fact that the unsub appears to have no qualms about going after professors in broad daylight—on a campus filled with students coming and going—tells me that the perp is either extremely confident that he's untouchable or is overconfident and getting reckless. Which is it?"

"That's the million-dollar question," Gayle said, taking a swig from her water bottle. "I wish I had the answer, believe me. If so, maybe I could use that info to help nail him to the wall. As it is, we're still trying to play catch-up with him. We're not exactly losing the battle, but we're not winning it either. At least not soon enough to have prevented yet another poor professor from losing her life at the hands of this monster."

"That's not our fault," Paula defended their actions. "We're police detectives, not magicians or mind readers. Like you, I feel absolutely terrible at the precious loss of life here. Just as everyone working in our departments does, I'm sure. But we can only work our butts off in investigating the murders and seeing where it takes us. I'm confident this will not turn into a cold case that is never solved. We won't let that happen, right?"

"Right." Gayle grinned. "Okay, so you've convinced me to not let it become too personal. The fact that we're both under pressure to crack the case doesn't mean it has to crack us. Not if we don't allow that to happen."

"We won't." Paula lifted her hand and they did a high five. "We're two strong women and more than capable of leading this investigation," she stressed. "I'm more determined than ever to finish what we've started, even if there are a few road bumps along the way that we just need to deal with."

"Me too." Gayle picked up the pace. "So, does that mean finishing whatever you've started with Neil Ramirez?"

Paula blushed. Was it that obvious? "Of course," she

admitted freely. "Wherever things are meant to go between us, they will."

Gayle took a breath and, gazing at her, asked thoughtfully, "Does that include going down the aisle again, should it ever come to that?"

Paula laughed. "We're nowhere near that point in our relationship," she had to say. At least she didn't think so. "But, generally speaking, yes, I think I would be willing to marry again, if the right person came along."

"Maybe that right person already has," she said brashly.

Or not, Paula told herself as she grabbed her water bottle. Far be it for her to try and read Neil's mind as to how far he wanted to take things. Maybe he didn't consider marriage in the cards for him. She would just have to wait and see which way the arrow pointed as they both weighed the future.

Paula imagined the same was true for Gayle. She knew the detective had a crush on Mike Davenport. Wisely, she didn't go after the happily married man. No reason to rock the boat and risk it sinking for all parties concerned. Besides, she was sure that Gayle would have no trouble attracting someone who was single and available. As long as it wasn't Neil, whom she had already said wasn't her type, but was very much Paula's.

THAT EVENING, Neil watched through his rearview mirror as Vinny Ortiz's Jeep Wagoneer came up behind him. The undercover agent emerged from the vehicle and headed toward Neil's Suburban. He glanced around to make sure neither had been followed—or was otherwise in danger of being exposed as they rendezvoused.

When Ortiz climbed into the passenger seat, he said

with an edge to his tone of voice, "Heard that another professor has been murdered on campus."

"Yeah." Neil took a ragged breath. "Wish it weren't true. Unfortunately, the Campus Killer seems to have struck again—seemingly becoming more and more emboldened to take down his prey."

"Too bad. This dude's definitely creating a stir around town, even in the gunrunning business. Craig Eckart is still lamenting over the murder of his girlfriend, Laurelyn Wong, by this serial killer."

"Nice to know that a man who sells and distributes illegal guns and ammo that kill people would be torn up when someone he's close to becomes a victim of violence." Neil made a sardonic face. "Cry me a river."

"I get where you're coming from, trust me," Ortiz said and ran a hand through his hair. "Eckart's definitely not one of the good guys. But you and I don't have the luxury of picking and choosing between creeps."

"Very true." Neil leaned back musingly. He needed Eckart to go down as much as the serial killer unsub. With Ortiz's work, they were about to make that happen. One victory at a time. "So, where do things stand?" he asked him anxiously.

"Everything's falling into place," Ortiz responded intently. "Eckart's got his dark web operation in full gear, with a variety of guns and ammo he's ready to make available to anyone who wants them. At the same time, he's built up a stash of firearms locally that he's prepared to distribute across the country to gang members, drug traffickers and others who want to purchase guns on the black market."

"Sounds like Eckart is ripe for the taking," Neil remarked knowingly.

"Yeah. It's definitely going to blow up in his face."

"What do you need from me?" Neil fixed his eyes on the undercover agent, aware that he had the most at stake in the dangerous operation.

"You need to let all the relevant parties know that it's crunch time," Ortiz told him tensely. "I'll text you just before, so everyone's in place to do what's needed to put the gunrunner out of commission."

"I'll take care of it," Neil promised, more than ready to do his part in harnessing the combined power of the ATF, Rendall Cove PD's Firearms Investigation Unit, with assistance from the Shays County Sheriff's Department, to put an end to this major arms trafficking enterprise.

"Okay." Ortiz gave him a solid nod and exited the vehicle.

As Neil started the ignition and then drove off, he only hoped this thing went down without a hitch. Beyond that, there was still the issue of trying to help Paula and company to put a perilous serial killer behind bars before the unsub could add to the string of victims he'd left behind.

Half an hour later, Neil showed up at Paula's front door. When she opened it, he said sheepishly, "Thought you could use some company."

Her lashes fluttered interestedly. "Oh, did you?"

He grinned, raising an arm to show what he was holding. "I brought white wine."

"Hmm…" She licked her lips and took the bottle. "Come in."

The moment Neil did, her cat, Chloe, pedaled across

the floor and affectionately rubbed herself on the leg of his pants. He laughed. "Looks like someone missed me."

Paula smiled nicely. "Guess you're starting to grow on her."

"Must be catching," Neil tossed back at her, feeling that she was growing on him in ways that cut deep into his heart and soul.

"Must be," she agreed without hesitation.

Chapter Twelve

On Friday morning, Paula was at her desk, going over the autopsy report on Charlotte Guthrie. As expected, the chief medical examiner determined that the associate professor of fisheries management's death was due to forceful asphyxia and ruled a homicide. Paula winced at the thought, hating the notion that doing something Charlotte obviously loved—running for fitness—should end this way.

Under other circumstances, I could have run into harm's way myself, Paula considered, while reading more of the mundane details of Eddie Saldana's official report on the decedent. The DNA removed from beneath Charlotte's fingernails was sent to the forensic lab for analysis, while the unsub remained at large.

Paula pulled up the surveillance video on her laptop of that section of campus, near the Cedar River. A male was seen running away from the area. Though the image was less than sharp, she could see that he was white, with short dark hair, tall and of average build, wearing a red jersey, blue jeans and black tennis shoes. It was enough to shake her foundation as a potential breakthrough.

Who are you? Paula asked suspiciously, believing

his identification could be crucial as a viable suspect in the investigation.

She headed over to the Department of Police and Public Safety's Forensic Science Lab, where Paula met with Forensic Scientist Irene Atai, who was in her thirties and petite, with brown hair in a braided bun and sable eyes behind oval glasses.

"Hey," Irene said from her workstation. "I think I know why you're here, Detective Lynley."

Paula gave a little smile. "So, what do you have for me on the DNA removed from beneath the nails of our latest homicide victim, Charlotte Guthrie?"

"Well, when the DNA sample was compared with the forensic unknown profile analyzed from below the nails of Professor Odette Furillo, it was a match." Irene's face lit up. "The two DNA samples belong to the same unsub," she asserted.

"Meaning the professors managed to scratch a single assailant who was present at both murders," Paula uttered, having anticipated this finding.

"Exactly," Irene said succinctly. "Though the unsub was able to avoid being clawed by the other victims, this certainly links two of the murders in building your case against the Campus Killer."

"You're right, it does." Paula knew they still needed more to really put the squeeze on the culprit. A confession would be nice. But since she doubted that would come voluntarily, the next best thing was to stitch together the hard evidence to make the unsub's guilt all but certain. "Did you come up with anything from the Crime Scene Investigation Unit's work at the site of Charlotte Guthrie's murder?"

"Yes," Irene responded with a lilt to her voice. "There was a partial footprint discovered in the dirt near the body that did not match the shoes worn by Professor Guthrie. Our analysis indicated that the print came from a male tennis shoe that was likely a size eleven. It may or may not have come from the killer," she cautioned, "given that, from what I understand, it's a popular area for runners on campus."

"That's true," Paula allowed. "But where there's even a little smoke, there could be fire ready to light up." She thought about the suspect on the surveillance footage who was wearing tennis shoes. Coincidence? Or a further indication of guilt?

IN HIS OFFICE, Neil touched base by video chat with the Grand Rapids field office's resident agent in charge, Doris Frankenberg, wanting to keep her up to speed on the arms trafficking investigation. In her early forties, with blond hair and highlights worn in a shaggy lob and green eyes behind contacts, she had made no secret of her desire to be promoted to the International Affairs Division. For his part, Neil was pulling for her to succeed. Even as he was thinking more and more about his own future with the organization, and whether or not it was truly where he belonged when looking down the line. Still pained by the death of his friend, Agent Ramone Munoz, Neil was well aware of how one's entire life could change in a flash. He didn't want to shortchange himself when it came to prioritizing the things he felt were most important in life. Such as finding love with someone he could grow old and have a family of his own with.

"Busting this international arms ring wide open

would be another coup for the ATF," Doris voiced with eagerness.

"Yeah, it would be great for the organization." Neil offered her a smile. "Even better would be to take the guns and ammo out of the hands of human traffickers, gang members, domestic assaulters, unstable lone shooters, etc."

"That too," she concurred. "Whenever Agent Ortiz gives the signal, we'll be ready to go in with everything we've got to take down Craig Eckart and his associates."

Neil nodded to that and talked a bit about the recent bomb threat at the university and the ongoing Campus Killer investigation.

Doris shot him a supportive look. "It's how we roll, Agent Ramirez," she said matter-of-factly. "Whatever the bad guys do, we—along with our law enforcement partners—are even better at stopping them. Even if the path can be downright bumpy at times."

"That's a good way to look at it," Neil told her, knowing that winning the war was what it was all about in the final analysis, in spite of losing a few battles along the way sometimes.

"It's the only way," she told him keenly. "Agent Munoz lost his life with that very philosophy in mind."

"I know." Neil thought about Ramone making the ultimate sacrifice, with his wife, Jillian, being left to raise his two girls alone. "I have to go," he told the resident agent in charge.

"All right." She flashed him a smile. "I'll see you soon back in the office."

"Yeah." He grinned weakly at her and ended the chat, while again contemplating his life as he looked ahead and behind at the same time. In each instance, what stood out was meeting Paula and not wanting to lose her, whichever direction he chose to take in his life.

PAULA WAS STANDING in Captain Shailene McNamara's office, briefing her on the latest in the investigation, when Mike Davenport interrupted. His expression was indecipherable before he said intently, "We just received a tip that the unidentified male in the surveillance video is Connor Vanasse, an undergrad at the university. I looked him up and saw that he's twenty-two years old and a junior, majoring in biochemistry and molecular biology in the College of Natural Science."

"Does he live on campus?" Paula asked curiously.

"Actually, he's living off campus in a nearby apartment building," Davenport said. "But he should be at school right now. I have his class schedule."

Shailene leaned forward from her wooden desk, practically rising out of her high-backed leather chair. "Find him," she ordered, moving her gaze between them. "If this Connor Vanasse is our Campus Killer, we don't want him to target any more professors before we can get him off the streets."

"I couldn't agree more," Paula said, peering at Davenport. "Do we know who the caller is?"

"No, it was anonymous," he replied.

She didn't put too much stock in that at the moment, as Paula understood that people knowledgeable about persons suspected of crimes were often reluctant to identify themselves for fear of reprisal from the suspect. Not wanting to get involved officially. Or, in some instances, preferring to keep a low profile from the often intrusive media that lived for stories on real-life serial killers.

"Let's go bring Connor Vanasse in," Paula told Davenport, adding, "I'll give Gayle and the Rendall Cove PD a heads-up on the suspect as a serious person of interest in our investigation." And Paula intended to do the same in keeping Neil in the loop on what seemed to be a major breakthrough in the case.

WHEN GAYLE RECEIVED the news alert that a credible suspect named Connor Vanasse was wanted for questioning, she wasted little time in heading for the Moonclear Apartments on Drake Drive where he lived. Was this actually their killer? A student? How had he managed to stay one step ahead of them—till now?

She pulled up to the complex and drove around the parking lot, looking for the white Toyota Camry registered to Vanasse. It was nowhere in sight. As Gayle had been told that the suspect was likely on campus at this hour, she assumed he wasn't in his apartment. But she was not taking any chances that Vanasse could somehow slip through the cracks.

With Paula and Davenport searching for the suspect at the university, Gayle left her car and rendezvoused with other detectives and officers from the Rendall Cove PD. A knock and then another on Vanasse's second-floor door produced no response. There were no sounds coming from within and no reason to believe he had been tipped off that they were looking for him, as Gayle preferred the element of surprise.

She left the officers there, in case Vanasse showed up, and to secure the scene, should they need to go in with a search warrant later. In the meantime, Gayle hopped back in her vehicle and headed to Addison University, eager to be in on a takedown of the suspect who was now at the top of the list as the possible Campus Killer terrorizing professors since June.

NEIL JUST HAPPENED to be in Horton Hall for a lecture, when he was informed by Paula via text that they had identified a suspect in the serial killer investigation, a third-year student named Connor Vanasse, who was thought to be in a different class in Horton Hall presently. Having been sent a student ID photograph of the suspect—he was white and square jawed with blue eyes and black hair in an Edgar haircut—and given a general description of being around six feet, two inches in height and of medium build, Neil sprang into action. Wanting to do his part to assist in detaining the person of interest till the school authorities could bring him in, he headed straight for the second-floor classroom where a lecture on the pharmacology of drug addiction was underway.

Entering the room up front, Neil gazed at the forty or so students seated, looking for anyone who resembled Connor Vanasse. No one stood out at first glance. He caught the attention of the slender, white-haired male professor in his sixties, who stopped lecturing on a dime as Neil approached him.

"Can I help you?" the professor asked curiously.

Flashing his ATF special agent ID away from the view of students, Neil whispered, "As part of an investigation, I'm looking for Connor Vanasse. I understand that he's one of your students, taking this class—"

The professor cocked a thickish white brow. "That's correct. Only I don't believe that Mr. Vanasse is attending class today, for whatever reason. You're free to check for yourself, though," he offered.

Though he had no reason to doubt the professor, Neil knew that, as a visiting professor, he was able to establish in his smaller classes who was in attendance and who was not. Still, given the stakes, he had to be on the safe side, so he peered again into the classroom, looking more carefully at each face. Finally, convinced that the person of interest was not present, Neil said levelly to the students, "I'm looking for Connor Vanasse. Does anyone know where I can find him?"

"Yeah, I think so," said a husky male student with dark hair in a two block cut and a Balbo beard. "At least later. Connor can be found most Friday nights hanging out at the Dillingers Club on Young Street."

"Thanks." Neil made a note.

"What's he done this time?" the student asked humorously, getting a laugh from other students. "Or should I ask?"

"Probably better that you don't," Neil said expressionless, believing it was best not to tip his hand. "Just need some information from him regarding a class I'm teaching." He wasn't sure they were buying that, but hoped it was enough to keep them from giving Connor Vanasse a warning that someone was looking for him.

Neil left the classroom just as Paula was walking toward him, along with Mike Davenport. He caught up to them and said, "Hey."

"Hey." Paula met his eyes. "Is Connor Vanasse in there?"

"Afraid not," Neil replied. "But short of finding him

in his next class for today, I have a lead on where we can find Vanasse tonight."

"Where's that?" Davenport asked with interest.

"According to a student, Vanasse spends his Friday nights at Dillingers, a nightclub on Young Street."

"I know the place," Davenport said. "It's known for being pretty rowdy."

"Not too surprised to hear that," Neil said, knowing that the college town had a reputation for partying, drinking and recreational marijuana usage.

Paula sighed and said, "It could also be the location where a serial killer has chosen to hide out."

Neil nodded and responded accordingly, "If so, we'll be there to flush him out."

AT 9:00 P.M., Paula showed her badge to the burly and bald-headed man at the door to the Dillingers Club to be let through without explanation. Neil, Gayle and Davenport followed suit and all went inside. As expected on a Friday night, it was packed with students and twentysomethings, milling about or standing in place with drinks in hand, chattering as loud music was piped through loudspeakers overhead.

"Why don't we fan out," Paula suggested to the others, knowing they were all carrying concealed weapons, with armed officers and sheriff's deputies waiting outside the club as backup. "If anyone spots Connor Vanasse, keep an eye on him and text the location."

"Will do," Gayle said tensely.

"If he's here, he might make a run for it if we're made," Davenport told them.

"We have to consider that he's armed and dangerous, assuming Vanasse is our killer," Neil pointed out.

Paula didn't discount that in the slightest and responded, "True, which is why we can't spook him. But
we also can't allow him to leave this building and en-
danger others."

Neil met her eyes. "If it's all the same to you, I think
I'll just tag along—as an added measure of precaution."

Holding his gaze, she understood that this was his way
of wanting to protect her as someone he cared about beyond their jobs in law enforcement. As she felt the same
way toward him, Paula nodded with approval, wanting
them both to get through this in one piece. "Let's head
out," she ordered and started moving through the crowd.

"Maybe we should have waited till Vanasse came
out," Neil said, trailing her close enough that Paula could
feel his warm breath on the back of her neck. "He'd be
easier to spot."

Though he made a good argument, she countered
with, "Given the situation we're facing with six victims, there's nothing easy about this. We need to catch
the perp wherever he happens to be—before someone
else gets hurt."

"Point taken. I'll follow your lead, Detective."

"Good." A tiny smile of satisfaction that they understood each other played on Paula's lips. As they moved
about, she peered through the throng of bar goers, looking for the suspect. She wondered if the intel on him
was faulty. Perhaps Vanasse had never shown up at the
club. Had yet to arrive. Or had already given them the
slip. Then Paula homed in on a man who was putting
the moves on an apparently interested attractive, cur-

vaceous blonde female. "That's him," Paula told Neil as she recognized the suspect from his picture.

"Yeah, I can see that," he agreed. Neil moved alongside her. "Why don't we see if Vanasse will come in peacefully...?"

Just as she agreed, Paula got an answer from the suspect, who spotted them and intuitively saw them as cops and abruptly shoved the young blonde woman at them and took off running.

Instinctively, Paula took off after him, with Neil hot on her heels. Along the way, they had to dodge others, clueless as to what was going on, as Paula felt her heart pounding rapidly. She saw that Gayle and Davenport were now also in pursuit of the suspect.

When Vanasse appeared to be reaching for something in the pocket of his jeans, Paula was about to remove her SIG Sauer pistol from its holster, when Neil stepped in front of her and leaped onto the suspect. Both fell to the ground, with Neil on top. In the blink of an eye, he had twisted Vanasse's arms behind his back and was joined by Davenport, who handcuffed him and declared toughly, "Connor Vanasse, we're taking you in on suspicion of murder—"

Paula reminded the suspect of his rights as he was lifted to his feet and the four of them led him off as quite possibly the Campus Killer.

Chapter Thirteen

Early Saturday morning, Paula sat beside Gayle in the interrogation room at the Department of Police and Public Safety. On the opposite side of the table, Connor Vanasse was seated, with a dour expression on his face. His hair was a bit longer than on the student ID but was still in the same style. She noted a small cut on his neck and wondered if that had come from Charlotte Guthrie, before he killed her. If so, the DNA sample collected upon his arrest last night would link him to both her death and that of Odette Furillo.

Admittedly, chomping at the bit to get the suspect to confess, Paula got right to the questioning, having already made it clear that he could stop this and request legal representation at any time. "Mr. Vanasse, as was indicated, we brought you here to see what you know about a murder that occurred on the Addison University campus on Wednesday—the victim being Associate Professor of Fisheries Management Charlotte Guthrie."

Vanasse's nostrils flared and he snorted, "I had nothing to do with what happened to that professor!"

"Is that so?" Gayle's tone was cynical. She narrowed her eyes at the suspect. "We have you on surveillance video near the scene of the crime. You care to explain that…?"

Vanasse flinched. "There's nothing to explain," he argued. "Yeah, I hung out a bit by the river like I always do. But I never saw Professor Guthrie. And I sure as hell didn't kill her."

"Why don't I believe you?" Gayle rolled her eyes. "I think you took note of her jogging pattern, and when an opportunity came, you attacked her."

"That's not true!" His voice snapped, and he gazed at Paula as if to help him out.

She wasn't inclined to do so, but did want to keep him talking. "Would you mind telling me how you got that cut on your neck?"

He shrugged. "Cut myself shaving."

"Is that so?" Her eyes narrowed with skepticism. "Does that happen often?" She thought again about the unidentified DNA found beneath the fingernails of not one, but two victims of the Campus Killer.

The suspect rubbed his nose. "Not so much," he claimed.

"What size shoe do you wear, Mr. Vanasse?" she asked politely.

"Eleven." His response was without hesitation, and he eyed her with misgiving. "Why do you need to know that?"

Paula gave him a direct gaze and answered bluntly, "A size eleven tennis shoe footprint was found near Professor Guthrie's body—" she glanced under the table at his tennis shoes "—much like the ones you're wearing."

Vanasse's expression grew ill at ease. "Hey, you can't plant this on me! I was never near her body, I swear."

Paula wasn't necessarily buying this. Far from it. "So, if you're innocent, why did you run when you saw us at the nightclub?" she challenged him.

He hesitated, running a hand nervously across his mouth and glancing from one detective to the other. Then, in a shaky voice, he said, "I panicked, okay. I've been dealing drugs on campus. Mostly prescription pills, weed and ketamine. I thought that's what this was all about and freaked."

As Paula weighed his response, Gayle dismissed it. She scowled and said to Vanasse, "That's not very convincing, in light of the circumstances. Why don't we go over this again. Why did you run away from the crime scene, in effect, if you had nothing to hide as it related to murdering a professor...?"

Vanasse stiffened but maintained his story. "I never knew it was a crime scene. All I did was walk alongside the river, smoking a joint, and left. That's it."

Glancing at Gayle and aware that Neil and Davenport were watching this in another room on a video monitor, Paula chewed on the suspect's claims and decided to shift gears a bit. "Let's talk about Mathematics Professor Odette Furillo—"

Vanasse lowered his brows. "What about her?"

"Did you know the professor?" Paula had gone over his classes for the entire school year and gotten no indication that he had taken classes with Professor Furillo. Or, for that matter, any of the deceased professors. But this didn't mean he hadn't become fixated from afar, or had otherwise targeted them.

"Not personally," he said wryly.

"You think this is amusing?" Gayle snapped at him.

"Of course not." Vanasse wiped the grin off his face. "No, I didn't know the professor—personally or otherwise—and I didn't kill her. If that's what you're thinking."

The thought has crossed my mind, and with good reason, Paula told herself, but said to him, "We're only here investigating a series of homicides, on and off campus, including the aforementioned professors. Getting back to Professor Furillo, do you have an alibi for the time of her death?"

Paula provided this information. The suspect was unable to account surely for his whereabouts, claiming that he had probably been on a drug high somewhere. The same pathetic story was used when asked where he was when professors Debra Newton, Harmeet Fernández, Kathy Payne and Laurelyn Wong were murdered by suffocation.

When Paula received a text message on her cell phone, she looked at it and whispered to Gayle, "We have the results of the DNA testing." As she reacted to this, Paula stood and, fixing her eyes on Vanasse, told him comically, "Don't go anywhere."

Outside the room, Paula called Irene Atai in the Forensic Science Lab for a video chat. "Hey, what did you find out?" Paula asked her attentively when she appeared on the screen.

Irene flashed her a look of excitement. "The DNA sample collected from the suspect, Connor Vanasse, was a direct match with the two DNA unknown profiles obtained from beneath the nails of professors Odette Furillo and Charlotte Guthrie."

"You're sure?" Paula asked this more out of habit

than questioning the validity of the DNA testing by the forensic analyst.

"Absolutely." Irene's voice lifted an octave. "Vanasse's DNA was definitely taken off him somewhere by both decedents. He's your unsub—"

"Thanks, Irene." Paula gave her a smile. "Good work."

After ending the chat, Paula considered this for a moment, before heading back inside the interrogation room, where she conveyed the information in Gayle's ear, who said gleefully, "We needed that."

It proved to be more than enough solid evidence to make their case for the suspect being the Campus Killer. Paula cast her eyes upon him and said doggedly, "Your DNA was found below the fingernails of Charlotte Guthrie and Odette Furillo, leading me to believe that you murdered the professors."

"No way!" Vanasse yelled an expletive, then said in fear, "I think this is where I ask for a lawyer—"

"I understand," she told him, knowing this was a wise move on his part. "You probably should lawyer up, at this point."

Upon ordering him to stand, Gayle cuffed him and said inflexibly, "Connor Vanasse, you're under arrest for the murders of Charlotte Guthrie and Odette Furillo, with other charges sure to follow."

NEIL WATCHED THE whole thing unfold in the monitoring room, along with Davenport, who remarked with confidence in his tone, "Looks like we've got him!"

"Seems that way." Neil couldn't knock the unmistakable DNA evidence that linked Vanasse to two of the serial murders. The MO of the killer and similarities of the homicides made it all but a certainty that they were perpetrated by the same person.

Connor Vanasse.

"Let's see if forensics can match the pattern from Vanasse's tennis shoe with the print found at the crime scene of Guthrie's murder," Davenport said.

"That would help," Neil admitted, in making the case for Vanasse as the Campus Killer.

"Yeah, definitely." The detective sighed. "This college town was certainly under siege as long as he remained on the loose," he uttered.

"I couldn't agree more." Having worked there these past few months, Rendall Cove had almost begun to seem like home to Neil. That was made more so by the presence of Paula in his life. The thought of ever losing that was something he suddenly found hard to even comprehend. Much less see put into practice.

When she and Gayle joined them in the hall, Neil could see the relief in Paula's face as she said with a catch to her voice, "Making an arrest in this case was imperative on so many levels."

"You're telling me," Gayle said and gave her a friendly little hug. "It was obvious that, when faced with the hard evidence of his guilt, Vanasse was completely tongue-tied."

Neil agreed somewhat, telling them, "Deny, deny, deny—or unwillingness to face up to one's own actions, even when they hardly have a leg to stand on to the contrary—is usually the case whenever a suspect is cornered like a rat and doesn't have anywhere else to turn, short of fessing up. Clearly, this was where Connor Vanasse found himself."

"Up a creek without a paddle," Davenport quipped, grinning.

Gayle laughed. "Hope the man's a good swimmer."

"Before we get too comfortable about Vanasse being put away for good," Paula stressed, "let's make sure that the Shays County prosecutor, Natalie Eleniak, plays ball in throwing the book at Vanasse."

"Give it time," Neil said prudently. "If Vanasse is the Campus Killer, he's not about to be let off the hook by the prosecutor or anyone else with a vested interest in seeing that justice is served."

"You're right." Paula showed her white teeth, which he loved seeing. "That process has only just begun, and I'll be around to see it through as long as it takes."

"Same here," Gayle pitched in. She eyed Neil curiously. "How about you, Agent Ramirez? Or will you have moved on to bigger and better things?"

He met Paula's gaze uncomfortably, knowing she was even more keen to hear his response. Though he didn't particularly like being put on the spot—with Gayle obviously knowledgeable about his romantic involvement with Paula—Neil didn't shrink away from the question. He couldn't do that. "You can be sure that whenever a verdict is reached in this case, I'll be on hand to watch the guilty party hauled off to prison." He knew that this wasn't necessarily what Paula wanted to hear but, for now, it was the most he could commit to while putting a few more important things in order in his life.

Neil sensed that Paula was all right with that for the time being.

WITH MORE THAN enough probable cause to believe that Connor Vanasse was responsible for multiple murders, a judge signed off on search warrants of the suspect's Toyota Camry and apartment—looking for any physical, forensic, demonstrative, digital and other evidence against Vanasse as it pertained to the Campus Killer investigation.

Paula and Gayle, along with other armed detectives and crime scene investigators, entered the suspect's apartment. It was only sparsely furnished and included two bedrooms and an open concept, stained brown carpeting and evidence throughout of illicit drugs and drug paraphernalia.

"A dealer and a druggie by his own admission," Gayle pointed out straightforwardly.

Paula concurred, but had to say, "That's the least of Vanasse's problems."

"True, even if they're all likely linked to one degree or another."

"Let's see if he can use the substance abuse and drug trafficking defense for murdering six professors," Paula said humorlessly. Once the all-clear signal was made, she put her gun back in its holster and continued surveying the premises.

By the time the team was through, having confiscated Vanasse's laptop, along with other potential evidence, taken photographs and headed out, Paula was satisfied that they had done their job as part of the overall investigation that figured to ultimately put Connor Vanasse away for the rest of his life.

ON SUNDAY, Paula went jogging with Neil at Rendall Creek Park. Though they spent the night together, with neither seeming to be able to get quite enough of the other, there was little talk about building bridges and crossing over them together, which she had agreed to. Instead, both settled into enjoying what they had and neither made any waves. That didn't prevent Paula from hoping there was a serious path forward that could give her the type of lasting love and committed relationship that had evaded her with Scott.

Neil, who had worked up a good sweat, broke her reverie when he said contemplatively, "I was thinking... What if Connor Vanasse didn't kill those professors?"

Paula arched a brow. "The evidence suggests otherwise."

"Evidence can sometimes be misleading. Distorted. Or even planted."

"What are you saying?" All she could think of was that he was implying that the police had set up Vanasse. Did Neil truly believe them capable of this?

"Whoa..." Neil made an expression as if reading her mind, as they continued to meander side by side through the groves of maple and eastern white pine trees. "I wasn't suggesting that the case against Vanasse was manufactured by the DPPS or PD," he made clear. "Nothing of the sort. I was only putting out there the notion that this all somehow seems just a little too cut-and-dried for me."

She narrowed her eyes at him. "We have Vanasse's DNA on two of the victims, a matching shoe print at one crime scene, security camera footage showing him fleeing the area and circumstantial evidence tying him to the murders. What more do you need, short of an outright confession?"

Neil sucked in a deep breath. "So, maybe I'm way off

base here." He paused. "There's still the motive to nail down. It's just something to think about."

Seriously, Paula mused. What was there to think about? Did he know something she didn't? "If Vanasse is innocent, who do you think is the Campus Killer?"

Neil took a long moment before favoring her with a determined look and replying candidly, "I have no idea. Just call it a gut instinct by a criminal profiler."

Though she respected his expertise, Paula wondered if he was searching for something that wasn't there. Or were his instincts spot on? Was it possible that Connor Vanasse, against all odds, was being railroaded? With the guilty party still on the loose? If so, why? And by whom?

Chapter Fourteen

On Monday morning, Neil followed his instincts that told him something felt off about the case against Connor Vanasse. The last thing he wanted to do was poke holes into the investigation and presumed guilt of the suspect. Or overstep his bounds as a criminal profiler and not one of the actual investigators, such as Paula—certainly not wanting to get on her bad side—who did all the dirty work in reaching the consensus on Vanasse.

But Neil went with his gut on this one. No harm. No foul. Right? Simply having a little chat with Vanasse would in no way hinder the progress of the case, which the Shays County prosecutor had yet to sign off on. *If Vanasse, who has maintained his innocence thus far, tries to play me, it won't work*, Neil told himself, from a metal chair as he watched the serial killer suspect enter the interview room at the Rendall Cove City Jail on Flagstone Avenue.

Wearing a horizontal black-and-white-striped jumpsuit while handcuffed, Connor Vanasse peered at him curiously and barked, "Who the hell are you?"

"Special Agent Ramirez," Neil told him. "Have a seat." He proffered his long arm toward the metal chair across the square wooden table.

Vanasse did as told, while Neil asked the tough-looking, bald headed, husky guard who accompanied him into the room to leave them alone. Though seemingly reluctant to do so, the guard left.

Vanasse cocked a brow. "So, why am I here?" he asked tentatively.

"I'd like to discuss the case against you." Neil got right to the point.

The suspect stared for a long moment and shrugged. "What's there to discuss?"

"Why did you do it?" Neil asked straightforwardly, peering across the table.

"I didn't do anything!" Vanasse stuck to his story. "Like I told the other detectives, and my lawyer, I had nothing to do with those murders."

Neil snickered. "If I had a dollar for every time a suspect claimed innocence when the evidence clearly suggested otherwise, I'd be a very rich man and probably living the good life in the Caribbean or Hawaii."

"It's the truth!" Vanasse snapped. "Whether you choose to believe it or not."

Not—at least not necessarily, Neil told himself. He asked point-blank, "Mind telling me how your DNA ended up beneath the fingernails of two professors who were suffocated to death?"

"I have no idea." Vanasse pursed his lips thoughtfully. "Must have been a mistake or something."

"Highly unlikely." Neil knew that while cross contamination was always possible with people coming and going across crime scenes, any notion that the DNA was not his would not fly. "Forensic testing puts you at the crime scenes and, by extension, that makes you the prime suspect in several other homicides. Do you have any thoughts of how it might have gotten there, since you allege you weren't there?"

Vanasse's shoulders slumped. "Maybe it was planted."

"Try again." Neil dismissed this at a glance. He regarded the small cut on the suspect's neck. "You said you cut yourself shaving. Is that true? And, if so, who had access to the blood other than yourself?"

Vanasse leaned back contemplatively and, after a moment or two, responded evenly, "Someone else cut me."

"Who?"

"Just a friend who was goofing around while we were getting high. It was no big deal."

"What's the friend's name?" Neil asked.

"Desmond Isaac," Vanasse answered matter-of-factly.

Neil's eyes widened at the name of his teaching assistant. "Desmond Isaac?" He repeated this as though having misunderstood.

"Yeah," Vanasse confirmed. "We were smoking weed and whatever…and when he was playing around with a switchblade, it accidentally nicked me."

How the hell did my TA wind up in the middle of this? Neil wondered, disturbed at the thought. "Where did this take place—and when…?"

"At my apartment—the same day that Professor Guthrie was killed."

"Who cleaned up the cut?" Neil asked curiously, in wanting to give Desmond the benefit of the doubt that his role was purely innocuous.

"We both did," Vanasse claimed. Then he changed this to say, "Actually, Desmond had a handkerchief that he used to wipe away the blood, then I grabbed a paper towel to finish it up." He frowned. "Wait a sec… You're not suggesting that Desmond—a friend—would use my blood…my DNA to set me up, are you?"

"I'm not suggesting anything of the sort," Neil argued, even if the possibility suddenly was weighing heavily on his mind. "Just looking for other ways that your DNA might have been beneath the nails of two victims, if you weren't scratched by them."

"I wasn't." Vanasse hunched his shoulders. "As I said, it must have been some kind of mix-up in the lab or something."

The *something* was what intrigued Neil more. "It's not possible that this would be the case in two different homicides that occurred days apart. Let's talk about Professor Odette Furillo," he said. "Since your DNA was also found underneath her nails, did you or someone else happen to cut you that day too?" He provided the day and time of death for Vanasse to ponder, aware that he had no solid alibi for any of the Campus Killer murders.

"Truthfully, I can't remember," he claimed. "I think I may've had a nosebleed that day."

"Did your buddy Desmond Isaac happen to be around at the time?" Neil asked intently.

"Yeah, probably. We've been hanging out a lot lately— doing drugs…and just kicking back between classes." Vanasse furrowed his brow. "Me and Desmond are cool. He wouldn't betray me like that. Or, for that matter, kill professors. To believe otherwise is just plain ridiculous!"

Neil's jaw clenched. "Would it be any more ridiculous to think that your good friend Desmond could plant your DNA at crime scenes rather than be arrested and charged with multiple murders that you claim you didn't commit?"

Vanasse snorted on a breath. "No, I guess not."

Admittedly, Neil still had his own doubts about pointing the finger at his TA as the Campus Killer. But as an ATF criminal profiler and visiting professor who needed to have an open mind, even when he was looking at the presumed serial killer, Neil was not about to give Desmond Isaac a free pass as a possible killer.

"What do you have to say about the fact that your size eleven tennis shoe, including dirt on the bottom, was a match for a print left at the crime scene of Charlotte Guthrie's murder?" Neil asked pointedly, narrowing his eyes at Vanasse.

"Can't explain it," he argued, "other than to say that half the dudes I know on campus are size eleven and wear the same brand of tennis shoes. Some of them even like to hang out on the banks of the Cedar River, like me. Does that make them guilty?"

"Does that include Desmond Isaac?" Neil couldn't help but wonder, even as he pictured the TA routinely wearing black tennis shoes that could have been a size eleven.

Vanasse wrinkled his nose. "You'll have to ask him that."

"Okay." Neil sighed thoughtfully and stood. "I'll be in touch."

"Does that mean you believe me?" Vanasse made a face. "That I'm being railroaded?"

"Let's just say I'm not as convinced as some that you killed those professors," Neil told him honestly. "Of course, if the evidence continues to prove me wrong, then you'll have your day in court."

Neil called the guard to come in and left the detainee there to ponder this.

"So, you're back!" Paula smiled while sitting at her desk as she took the video call from her friend, Josie Woods, recognizing the floor-to-ceiling windows overlooking New York City in Josie's Wall Street office.

"Wish it weren't true but, unfortunately, all good things must eventually come to an end." Josie pouted. "It was fun while it lasted though."

"I'll bet." Paula still dreamed of going to Hawaii herself someday—perhaps with Neil, if things worked out between them as she hoped would be the case. "So, what's happening in the Big Apple?"

She listened for a few minutes as Josie droned on about business meetings and her millionaire boyfriend Rob's latest obsession with rare collectibles. Paula had just skimmed the surface on her latest investigation and begun to touch on her relationship with Neil, when her cell phone buzzed and she saw that he was the caller. "I need to take this," she told Josie, who smiled with understanding before they disconnected.

Paula hoped to get out to New York to visit soon as she answered the phone. "Hey, there. What's up?"

"As out there as this sounds, I think my teaching assistant Desmond Isaac may have set up Connor Vanasse to take the rap as the Campus Killer," Neil said tonelessly.

"What?" Paula's lower lip hung down as she pressed the phone to her ear with disbelief.

"I went to see Vanasse," he confessed.

"You did?"

"Yes. I wanted to clear up some things that, as a profiler, rubbed me the wrong way during his interrogation."

Neil breathed into the phone. "According to Vanasse, he and Desmond did drugs together."

Paula jutted her chin. "And that proves what?"

"Vanasse says that on the same day that Charlotte Guthrie was killed, Desmond accidentally cut Vanasse's neck with a switchblade when toying around—and used a handkerchief to wipe the blood. Desmond could have technically rubbed Vanasse's DNA beneath Guthrie's nails after he suffocated her to death," Neil argued.

"You really believe that's possible?" Paula asked doubtfully.

"It's not impossible to think that someone clever enough—a criminology student, for example, with knowledge of crime scene techniques, DNA evidence, planting evidence and such—could have found an unsuspecting scapegoat to take the fall for a string of murders and allow the true culprit to go unpunished."

"But what about the DNA found beneath Odette Furillo's nails?" Paula questioned. "Are you saying this was a setup as well?"

"Why not?" Neil answered tersely. "Vanasse claims that he can't remember for certain if he had a nosebleed or how he ended up losing blood the day Furillo was murdered. But he does think that he may have been hanging out with Desmond at the time. This might all be nothing more than happenstance," Neil indicated, "but my instincts are telling me otherwise."

"Meaning what exactly?" she asked him keenly, knowing that reopening the investigation—and coming away with a different conclusion—would still need more than just a hunch and questionable circumstances.

"For starters, I think you need to go through the surveillance videos—before and after the murders," he told her. "Some serial killers like to come back to the scene of their crimes. If that's true here, we might expect to see Desmond lurking about here or there, knowing he wasn't on our radar. Basically, revisiting everything you have in the case against Connor Vanasse that may open up the possibility that he's not the Campus Killer. If there are no loose ends or discrepancies to that effect, then Vanasse is your killer."

And if he's not, I can't let an innocent man go down, she told herself, wanting to keep an open mind against the present trajectory of the investigation. "All right," Paula agreed. "And what will you do next to check out your TA?"

"Whatever is necessary to see if he's been playing us all and is truly a stone-cold killer," Neil said with an edge to his voice.

WHEN TEACHING ASSISTANT Rachelle Kenui walked into his office, Neil was sure she believed this was a routine visit pertaining to her duties for one of his classes. He only wished it was that simple. As was the case, this was anything but simple, if his fears about Desmond held water.

"Have a seat," Neil offered, as he leaned against a corner of his desk. Once she was on the black accent chair, he asked her knowingly, "I'm sure you heard that there has been an arrest made in the Campus Killer investigation?"

"Yes. The news spread like wildfire across campus." Rachelle pushed up her gold retro horn-rimmed glasses. "It was a real relief to know that the killer's behind bars."

Neil regarded her. "Do you know Connor Vanasse?"

"Not directly," she replied. "I've seen him around campus, but that's as far as it went."

"Do you know if Desmond knows him?"

"I couldn't say." Rachelle shrugged. "If so, he never shared it with me."

Neil paused musingly. "I need to know the nature of your relationship with Desmond. Are you two just colleagues or…?"

"We're friends," she responded quickly. "We've been spending time together lately, but it's nothing serious." She hesitated. "Why are you asking about this? Did you hear something…?"

"To be clear, what you and Desmond do outside the department is your business," Neil needed to say. "This has nothing to do with that, per se… As part of the Campus Killer Task Force, I have some concerns involving Desmond."

Rachelle's lashes fluttered. "What type of concerns?"

Gazing at her, Neil said sharply, "I have reason to believe that Desmond not only hung out with Connor Vanasse, but may have set him up for the murders…"

"Seriously?" She pushed her glasses up again. "How's that even possible?"

"You'd be surprised," he told her forthrightly. "People can be capable of almost anything, if given the right tools, cunning and motivation." Neil gazed at her. "Did Desmond ever talk to you about the Campus Killer murders or any of the professors as victims?"

Rachelle thought about it and said, "Well, yeah, he— or we—talked about the murders as they happened. I figured his interest was that of a criminology grad student, wanting to pick my brain and vice versa on the dynamics of the murders. I don't know if I can say he had a particular fixation on the Campus Killer's crimes."

"Did Desmond ever ask you to be his alibi?" Neil wondered.

"No, not that I can recall."

That doesn't mean he wouldn't have, were such an alibi needed, Neil thought. He angled his face and asked if she was with Desmond at the times the victims were believed to have been killed—giving these to her one by one. In each case, Rachelle asserted that they were not together, taking away any potential line of defense for the TA, which now had Neil believing there could be a far darker side to him than ever imagined.

"Do you really think that Desmond could be capable of such heinous actions—including pinning this on someone else?" she questioned with incredulity.

"That's what we need to find out," he replied, a catch to his tone. "Was there anything at all that stood out to you with Desmond where it concerned the Campus Killer investigation?"

She sucked in a deep breath, and her voice shook while saying, "Actually, there was one thing I found kind of weird... After we were introduced to Detective Lynley, Desmond did comment that he had the hots for her—saying that she reminded him of someone he once dated and wished he could have another shot at. I had the strange feeling that he would have welcomed the opportunity to go out with the detective, if he had the chance."

Neil cringed at the thought of someone like Desmond trying to put the moves on Paula. Had he tried to romance any of the Campus Killer victims? Was he the guilty party? Instead of the one languishing in jail?

I have a bad feeling that Desmond is guilty as hell, Neil told himself. And just might decide to go after Paula to fulfill some dark and deadly fantasies. He wasn't about to let that happen.

After Rachelle left the office, Neil called Mike Davenport and said gravely, "Hey, I need you to get me everything you have on the anonymous tip that pointed the finger at Connor Vanasse as the purported killer of Charlotte Guthrie and, by virtue, the Campus Killer."

"Uh, okay," Davenport hummed. "You wanna clue me in on what this is all about...?"

"I'd be happy to. I have strong reason to believe that one of my teaching assistants may have set up Vanasse to take the rap," Neil told him sadly. "Now I just need to prove it..."

And make sure that justice didn't take the wrong turn in bringing the hammer down on the Campus Killer.

Chapter Fifteen

Paula studied the surveillance video taken outside the Gotley Building the morning after Odette Furillo was murdered. She zoomed in on one of the bystanders. *It's him*, she told herself, recognizing the face.

Desmond Isaac.

He appeared calm and collected, while fitting in, almost unnoticeable. His gaze was constantly shifting—as though on guard, even as he presented himself as an innocent onlooker in the wake of a homicide.

Was this a serial killer returning to the scene of one of his crimes?

Paula considered that, according to Neil, this was part of the MO of some killers, who liked hiding in plain view at crime scenes as part of some vicarious thrill of pulling one over on their pursuers. *Is that the sick game you're playing here, Desmond?* she mused absorbedly. Was Connor Vanasse the perfect mark for him to set up?

Going through more security camera footage, Paula saw in at least two other instances at or near crime scenes of other victims of the Campus Killer, Desmond Isaac's face showed up. How had they missed this? Was he merely a true crime addict?

Or a lethal killer, who got his kicks out of pushing the limits of exposure and apprehension?

As she contemplated this, Davenport came into her office, his expression unreadable. "What is it?" Paula asked perceptively.

"Looks like we have a problem…"

"Would that problem have anything to do with Desmond Isaac?"

Davenport nodded, his brow creased. "Neil phoned me an hour ago, asking for info about the anonymous call we received that identified Connor Vanasse as the unsub on video seen running from the area where Charlotte Guthrie was killed."

Paula shifted in her chair. "What did you learn?"

"Well, for starters, the caller used a burner phone," Davenport told her. "Given the obvious implications pertaining to our case against Vanasse, I obtained a search warrant to track the location of the phone. It pinged from inside the Quinten Graduate Center. According to Neil, his graduate student TA Desmond Isaac lives in this dormitory—and was believed to have been there at the time the call was placed."

Though this wasn't necessarily an indictment of guilt in being a serial killer in and of itself, Paula felt that this only added to the case that was quickly starting to build against the teaching assistant. And move away from Connor Vanasse.

"Ramirez made a compelling case for Isaac setting up his drug buddy, Vanasse, by planting his DNA to take the fall as the Campus Killer," Davenport remarked, leaning against the wall. "Seems like Rachelle Kenui, his other

TA, has some interesting things to say about Isaac that lends credence to him being our killer."

"There's more," Paula told him. "Come take a look at the surveillance videos I pulled up that show Desmond lurking about at more than one of the murdered professors' crime scenes."

After digesting this, Davenport muttered strongly, "We need to bring Desmond Isaac in for questioning."

"I agree. The sooner, the better." The last thing Paula wanted was to let the latest—and perhaps most cunning—person of interest somehow worm his way out of the weeds as a killer, without being held accountable for his crimes. If, as she was beginning to believe, Desmond Isaac proved to be the Campus Killer. Still very much at large. And perilous.

Once they took this to the captain, she didn't hesitate to come on board in the fight for justice. And against an injustice. In Paula's mind, these were one and the same. Desmond had a lot to answer for. But would he play ball? Or try to climb out of a hole that seemed to be getting deeper and deeper for the TA?

WHEN NEIL GOT the word that the anonymous tip came from the Quinten Graduate Center on campus, his focus on Desmond Isaac grew more intense. As it was, the timing of the call, using a burner phone, corresponded within minutes to a call Neil made to his TA's cell phone number. He recalled Desmond telling him that he was at the dorm when the call was made. Coincidence?

I don't think so, Neil told himself, as he left his office. Not when combined with other damning evidence against his TA.

He headed to Jamison Hall where, according to Associate Professor George Tyler, Desmond was currently in Tyler's Criminal Justice Behavior and Ethics class. Given his strong suspicions toward him, Neil found it almost laughable in a humorless way that Desmond would be enrolled in the class, contrary to his own suspected behavior as a purported serial killer.

After driving to the building, Neil went inside and, though armed, hoped Desmond would allow himself to be taken into custody peacefully. But he had to be prepared that the killer suspect could resist. And even potentially use the professor or other students as shields to hide behind.

All of that proved to be a moot point when Professor Tyler sent Neil a text, just before he entered the classroom, to report that Desmond Isaac had abruptly left the class moments earlier. After verifying this, Neil searched for his TA, believing that he must have used the back stairwell to escape. Had he been tipped off? Or had the alleged Campus Killer developed a sixth sense as part of his cold and calculating psyche, warning him of danger?

While heading back to his office, Neil notified Paula and other members of the team that Desmond had managed to evade him.

WITH NEWS THAT Desmond Isaac was still on the loose, Paula drove with Davenport to the Quinten Graduate Center, equipped with arrest and search warrants for the individual now suspected of being a suffocation-style serial killer.

"This case keeps getting weirder and weirder," Davenport commented from behind the wheel with a frown on his face.

"I know." Paula pursed her lips. "The pieces did seem to fit where it concerned Connor Vanasse," she noted. "Which made him the perfect patsy for the criminology graduate student, Desmond Isaac."

"Yeah," the detective concurred. "Except his master plan has started to unravel."

"Which makes him all the more dangerous, with his back suddenly against the wall," Paula said thoughtfully, as they drove into the Quinten Graduate Center parking lot.

After checking the lobby and cafeteria for any signs of the suspect and finding none, they headed for his fifth-floor room in the east wing and knocked, to no avail.

Davenport sighed with annoyance. "Doesn't look like he's come back here."

"Unless he wants us to believe that's the case," Paula said suspiciously. "Why don't you stand guard here and keep an eye out for him. I'll go get someone to let us in…"

"All right."

Down at the front desk of the dorm, Paula flashed her identification at the hazel-eyed slender young female attendant, with thick hair in a platinum blonde balayage style, and told her, "I'm Detective Lynley. I have a search warrant to get inside the room of Desmond Isaac."

The young woman glanced at the search warrant and sighed with indifference. "What's he done?"

"Maybe nothing," Paula answered dispassionately, though strongly suspecting it was just the opposite.

She rolled her eyes. "Whatever," she said dryly, phoning someone from management to meet Paula at the room.

Moments later, they were inside the single occupant room and found it empty. Judging by the untidiness, it appeared as though Desmond had come and gone in a hurry. Missing was his laptop and any cell phones. Donning a pair of nitrile gloves, Paula searched the suspect's desk and chest of drawers for anything that might be visibly incriminating in the case. All she found was drug paraphernalia, a bag of marijuana and a small amount of illicit opioids.

"You may want to take a look at what's in the closet." Davenport got her attention.

When Paula walked to the closet, the sliding door was open all the way and hanging clothes were pushed to one side. On the back wall were photographs of all the victims of the Campus Killer, printed out from a computer. It gave her a chill. "Who keeps pictures of a serial killer's victims hidden inside the closet?"

"Someone who gets his kicks out of collecting and looking at them whenever the mood suits him," Davenport answered matter-of-factly, wearing gloves. "Such as the Campus Killer."

She wrinkled her brow. "I was afraid you'd say that," she moaned.

"There's something else." His voice dipped uneasily.

Her eyes turned to his. "What…?"

"This." Davenport moved the clothes to the other side of the closet to reveal a school newspaper clipping on the wall of Paula and Gayle during the investigation. "Looks like the creep has a fascination for female detectives too…"

Paula gulped as another chill ran through her at the thought of her or Gayle being suffocated to death by

Desmond. She voiced firmly what surely went without saying, "We have to find him—"

"I know." Davenport favored her with a supportive look.

A BOLO was put out for Desmond Isaac and the black Mazda CX-30 the murder suspect was believed to be driving.

GAYLE WAS IN disbelief that they apparently had the wrong person in jail in Connor Vanasse. The persuasive evidence—if you could call it that—while compelling, to say the least, had been an attempt by the real Campus Killer to point them in the wrong direction. Hard as it was to believe that Desmond Isaac had nearly pulled this off, she trusted Paula, Mike and Neil in the investigating they'd done that led them to conclude Neil's teaching assistant was actually the true culprit. He'd used his grad student studies in criminology and evidence manipulation to make Vanasse the fall guy.

Equally disturbing to Gayle, as she drove on Ellington Street at Addison University in search of the suspect's vehicle, was the thought that Isaac had evidently had her and Paula on his target list, along with the professors. Would the so-called Campus Killer have really come after them, while trying to finger Vanasse as the serial killer? Or had Isaac fully intended to kill her and Paula beforehand, but never had the right opportunity to do so?

Whatever the case, Gayle was on guard for as long as the suspect was on the loose. She had no wish to die before her time and by his hand, any more than Paula, as both had too much to live for. In Paula's case, she needed the longevity to move things along with Neil in the proper direction. And for herself, Gayle was sure there was someone out there for her. She only needed to stay alive to find him.

Her reverie ended when she spotted the black Mazda CX-30 parked crookedly across the street, next to the Intramural Sports Building. Knowing it matched the description of the suspect's vehicle, Gayle did a U-turn and pulled her Ford Escape up behind the Mazda. It appeared to be empty. She ran the license plate and saw that the car was indeed registered to a Desmond K. Isaac.

Gayle called it in and requested backup. She got out of her car and drew her weapon, in case the suspect was hiding inside the Mazda. Approaching carefully, she determined that there was no one inside. Scanning the area, she decided that Isaac had ditched the vehicle and was on the run. But where to, as a desperate man who may be even more dangerous if he believed he had nothing to lose?

NEIL LEARNED THAT Rachelle Kenui had texted Desmond Isaac, asking that he turn himself in. Rachelle believed she was helping facilitate a peaceful surrender of her fellow teaching assistant. For that, Neil did not fault her. Unfortunately, giving Desmond a heads-up seemed to have backfired as, by all accounts, he was making a conscious effort to avoid capture.

Of even more concern to Neil was the clear indication that Paula, along with Gayle, was in the serial killer suspect's crosshairs. When combining Rachelle's intuition about Desmond with the proof Paula and Davenport had found in Desmond's dorm room of his fixation on Paula—in spite of the attempt to lay blame for the

Campus Killer murders on Connor Vanasse—Neil was even more fearful that Desmond might go after Paula.

I can't allow him to hurt her, Neil told himself, as he headed out of Horton Hall, having just received word that the suspect's vehicle had been found abandoned nearby. Paula was on her way over to his office, where Neil had hoped to strategize more with her in putting the finishing touches on this case, once and for all. With Desmond on the loose and in the area, Neil didn't want to take any chances that he might actually show up at the building, for whatever reason.

Desperate people could do desperate things, Neil knew. Desmond Isaac certainly fit into that category. Along with being a cold and calculating serial killer, as it now appeared was all but certain.

All Neil could think of at the moment was that he loved Paula too much to let Desmond take what they could have away from them. But when Paula was not responding to calls or texts on her cell phone, Neil feared that he may already be too late to stop his soon-to-be former TA.

Chapter Sixteen

Paula wondered how Desmond Isaac had managed to slip through the cracks earlier in their investigation, as she headed over to see Neil to compare their notes and coordinate their efforts toward bringing his teaching assistant in for questioning. With the signs all pointing toward his guilt and Connor Vanasse being set up to take the fall as the Campus Killer, it was imperative that they put an end to this. Before Desmond Isaac could do more damage.

In Paula's mind, that included going after her or Gayle, as the hidden newspaper clipping inside his closet seemed to imply. The fact that Desmond had ditched his car on campus meant that he was likely on foot. Though she couldn't rule out that he had grabbed a bicycle or moped in a desperate means to evade capture. With the BOLO alert, there were few places he could hide on campus, or in Rendall Cove, for that matter. This meant that his arrest was imminent.

But until such time, Paula knew neither she nor Gayle could or should rest easy. *I'm sure Neil feels the same way*, Paula told herself, pulling into the parking lot of Horton Hall. With the connection between Desmond as his TA and the School of Criminal Justice, Neil had added incentive to want him off the streets and the investigation into the Campus Killer finally brought to a close the correct way.

Beyond that, Paula found herself wondering where that would leave her and Neil on a personal level. She wanted so much more with and from him—the man she had fallen hopelessly in love with—and couldn't imagine their momentum hitting a brick wall once his work as a visiting professor had come to an end. But that would have to wait, with other matters more pressing at the moment.

When she emerged from her car, Paula realized that her cell phone was buzzing. She pulled it from the pocket of her high-rise flare pants and saw that it was Neil, bringing a smile to her face. *Can't wait to see you, too*, she thought.

Only before she could answer the call, Paula heard a low but steady male's voice say intently, "I wouldn't answer that if I were you, Detective Lynley."

Paula looked into the icy eyes of Desmond Isaac and then down at the Beretta 3032 Tomcat Kale Slushy pistol in his hand, pointed at her, recognizing the .32 ACP gun from a previous case she had worked on. She resisted the urge to respond to the call and tell Neil she was in danger, and instead furrowed her brow at the suspected serial killer and said sharply, "Just what do you think you're doing, Desmond?"

"I'm sure you're well aware what's going on, Detective Lynley." His brows twitched. "You and your colleagues, thanks to Prof Ramirez, are looking for me… Well, it's my lucky day—you've found me. I'll take that phone from you now."

How had he managed to remain on the loose? Paula peered at him. "You're making a big mistake, Desmond."

"You'll be making a bigger one, if you don't do as I asked!" he countered menacingly. "The phone, please…" She did as he requested, handing it over, then watched as Desmond tossed it into a clump of common witch hazel shrubs. "Now I need your gun, Detective!"

As Paula weighed whether or not she should comply, or even attempt to take out the firearm and use it in self-defense, Desmond had taken it upon himself to remove the SIG Sauer P365 semiautomatic pistol from the holster that was tucked just inside her beige one-button blazer. He placed it in the pocket of his black fleece shirt jacket and said, "Next, I need you to help me get off this campus—in your car," he snorted.

"If you want the car, take it," she spat, ready to hand him the key fob.

"I don't think so." His expression hardened. "You're driving."

Paula hesitated, knowing that getting into any car with him—even her duty vehicle—was not in her best interests. She wrinkled her nose defiantly at Desmond. "Seriously? Are you really going to add to your troubles by kidnapping a police detective?" Even in asking this, Paula knew that it was not likely going to move the needle in her favor for someone who had nothing to lose at this point of desperation. She was even more concerned about what he might have in mind for her, given what she had seen in the closet of his dormitory room.

Desmond gave a derisive chuckle. "I'm way past wondering if it's a smart move or not, don't you think? As it is, Detective Lynley, you've really left me with no other choice, given the rather precarious predicament you and the other cops hunting me have put me in." He aimed the gun at her face and said forcefully, "Let's go…"

Knowing he had her at a disadvantage, Paula didn't make any waves just yet, if only to buy time without being shot. She began heading toward her Mustang Mach-E, hoping that someone—if not Neil—would spot Desmond as a passenger in her car and prevent them from getting too far. Short of that, she needed to be prepared to do anything necessary to come out of this alive.

Or die trying.

NEIL HAD JUST come out of the building when he spotted Paula's white Mustang leaving the parking lot, with her in it. At first glance, he found this odd. Where was she going? Why hadn't she responded to his calls or texts?

Then he saw that she wasn't alone in the car. As it turned onto Creighten Road, it became apparent to Neil that the occupant in the passenger seat was Desmond Isaac.

His heart skipping a beat, Neil knew instinctively that his former teaching assistant had taken Paula against her will. Most likely at gunpoint. Desmond was hoping to dodge the dragnet for his capture by using her as an escape mechanism.

Then what?

Neil had good reason to fear that Desmond would like to add Paula to his victim count before this was through, given his track record and knowledge that they were on to him. *Not if I have any say in it*, he told himself determinedly, as Neil raced toward his own car. He was well aware that allowing them to leave the campus would place Paula in even greater danger. The alternative of stopping this from happening at risk to her life would undoubtedly get under Desmond's skin too, should he fail. It was a chance Neil was willing to take, with stakes that couldn't be higher for the woman he loved.

Along with everything they dreamed of that was within their grasp. So long as a serial killer didn't destroy it, as he had so many other dreams.

Getting on his cell phone, Neil told Davenport, "Desmond Isaac's got Paula."

"What?"

"He abducted her in broad daylight from outside Horton Hall and forced her to drive him in her vehicle." Neil was certain. "They're headed down Creighten Road."

Davenport muttered an expletive, then said solidly, "I'll notify patrols to set up roadblocks at Grand Avenue, Rockfield Road, and Notter Street. They won't get very far."

I'll believe it when I see it, Neil thought, not taking anything for granted where it concerned the cunning killer grad student. He got into the car, started the ignition and said, "We need to bring in a SWAT team, K-9 unit—and even a hostage negotiator in case that's necessary."

"I'll get right on it," Davenport promised, seemingly masking his own concern for Paula's safety. "I'll let Gayle and the Rendall Cove PD know what's going on," he added, and Neil was certain this was for his benefit, so as to present a united front in tackling this latest turn in the investigation.

"Yeah," he told the detective simply and drove onto the street. "I'm going after them."

"You really think that's a good idea?" Davenport questioned. "If you're made by Isaac, there's no telling how he might react…"

Though this consideration was surely on his mind, Neil responded straightforwardly, "And if I do nothing and something bad happens to Paula, apart from being nabbed by a man we think has already murdered six females, I'd never be able to live with myself."

As if he understood that Neil was speaking from the heart in his words, Davenport told him, "Do what you need to." He paused. "We'll get through this."

Neil disconnected. He sure as hell was not leaving that to chance. Something told him that Paula felt exactly the same way, as he sped down the street until he caught sight of her vehicle.

PAULA SPOTTED IN the rearview mirror a car that had seemed to be moving fast, but then slowed down. As if to give them some room.

Neil.

How did he know? Did he somehow find her phone?

It meant Neil had notified others and, as such, help was on the way. But not necessarily soon enough to keep her gun-toting passenger from becoming suicidal and taking her with him.

I have to distract him, Paula thought as she glanced at Desmond. He was holding the gun on her and definitely jittery, as she rounded the traffic circle and headed onto Aspen Lane. She sucked in a deep breath and said, "So, what was this all about, Desmond? Why did you kill those professors? What did they ever do to you?"

He gave an amused chuckle, glancing out the side

window and back. "What did they do to me?" he asked mockingly. "Well, other than Debra Newton—who decided I wasn't good enough for her, too young, too weird or whatever, and had to pay the ultimate price—the other professors had to die because they thought the world revolved around them. At least that was how I took it while observing them from afar. Someone needed to knock them off their pedestals. I volunteered for the job," Desmond boasted and laughed.

So full of yourself, Paula thought as she drove. "Why kill them off and on campus?" she asked curiously. "Or was this all just a big game to you, sadistic as it was?"

He jutted his chin. "Yeah, I suppose you could say it was a game of sorts," he admitted. "I definitely got my kicks out of suffocating some of them to death on campus and others elsewhere. But, truthfully, I also wanted to keep you guys off balance by mixing things up a bit. Beyond that, the laws of average told me that killing them all on campus, which was my natural inclination, was only asking for trouble, with surveillance cameras, too many people out and about, and so forth."

Paula shook her head in disgust. "Did you really think you would get away with this," she decided to challenge him, "by setting up Connor Vanasse to take the fall for what you did?"

"Uh, yeah, I thought it was a good possibility," he admitted. "I laid out my game plan to near perfection. Taking out one victim after another, using what I'd learned as an Addison U criminology graduate student and basic common sense to put this into motion." Desmond laughed with satisfaction. "It was also admittedly good research for my thesis on homicides in society and its impact on local communities." He chuckled again. "As for poor Connor, it wasn't all that difficult to take advantage of his distractions with taking and dealing drugs to collect his DNA and plant it on a couple of the victims. The nosebleed Connor had gave me the perfect excuse to relieve him of some of the blood to smear beneath the nails of Professor Odette Furillo. Later, I pretended to cut Connor accidentally and insisted upon cleaning up the blood. Unbeknownst to him, I kept enough to rub below the nails of Professor Charlotte Guthrie."

"That's sick," Paula hissed at him, trying to fathom the lengths he was willing to go to as a serial killer. "Too bad it's all fallen apart now."

Desmond sneered. "Honestly, I wondered how long it would take you and the others to figure out who was truly behind the killings—if ever. Then Prof Ramirez had to interject himself into the case, thanks to you, and used his skill set as a profiler to piece everything together."

Paula glanced at the rearview mirror and saw that Neil was still lying back, undoubtedly not wanting to rock the boat prematurely. "Don't blame him for what you did," she said snippily. "That's all on you—"

"And I own up to it." He chuckled nastily. "At least now I do. With the cat out of the bag, I might as well enjoy the glory of being the Campus Killer—who's not quite through yet…"

He kept the gun on her, as if to prove his point. This told Paula what she already sensed. She would not come out of this alive. Not if Desmond had his way. She prayed that wouldn't be the case.

NEIL WATCHED AS Paula approached the roadblock on Grand Avenue, then took a sharp turn onto Beasley Road, headed toward Rockfield Road. It too would be cut off, preventing Desmond Isaac's escape with his captive. With nowhere to go, what might the suspected serial killer do next?

The thought made Neil cringe as he continued to trail them from a safe distance, though he seriously doubted that anyone with Desmond's cunning and awareness would be kept from knowing they were being followed for long. When backed into a corner, he might go on the attack at any time. With Paula being left to fend for herself.

I trust that she's capable of doing whatever it takes to survive, Neil told himself. He just wasn't nearly as certain it would be enough against the likes of a heartless serial killer, seemingly wanting to win at any and all costs.

Putting on his criminal profiler hat, Neil found himself sizing up more of the negative character traits of his ex-teaching assistant. He saw Desmond as the classic narcissist, somehow believing himself to be smarter than everyone else—and certainly more bloodthirsty in his thought patterns. From what he knew about him, as seen in a new light, Neil was sure that Desmond also suffered from borderline personality disorder and antisocial personality disorder.

It went without saying that his former TA had proven himself to be a sadist, Neil concluded. Meaning that Desmond would have no sympathy for Paula, no matter how Neil sliced it. He had to find a way to save her, as well as put a stop to Desmond's unnatural thirst for murder.

"LOOKS LIKE WE'VE got company," Desmond said with a sneer as he looked behind them. "Professor Neil Ramirez. Or should I say ATF Special Agent Ramirez? Why am I not surprised? He seems to have a real knack for continuing to stick his nose in my business."

Paula saw no reason to deny the obvious. "All of the law enforcement personnel involved in this case are on to you, Desmond," she pointed out matter-of-factly. "Why do you think the roads leading off campus are being blocked?"

Desmond grumbled as he looked ahead and saw patrol cars forming a barrier in front of Rockfield Road. He muttered an expletive, then barked defiantly, "If you want me—come and get me!"

"It's over, Desmond." Paula hoped to convince him to quit while he was ahead. And while both of them were still alive. "There's no way out of this for you. Why don't you let me pull over. Just give yourself up and no one else has to get hurt."

"By *no one*, you mean yourself?" he snickered.

She eyed him keenly. "I mean either one of us," she offered succinctly. "Killing me means killing yourself. You don't want that. Think of all you could offer from your experiences. Let's end this now!"

He cackled, the gun still firmly aimed in her direction. "I don't think so. I have a better idea. Why don't we bypass the patrol cars up there and take a little drive around the circle to the Campus Arboretum...and wait for Prof Ramirez to join us."

Paula recoiled at the thought of leading Neil into a deadly trap. But given that Desmond was unstable enough to shoot her right then and there, she didn't see where she had much choice. Other than to go along with the Campus Killer, knowing that Neil and the rest of the team were converging on them to end the threat.

One way or the other.

NEIL WAS SURPRISED to see that Paula had circumvented the roadblock by turning onto Leland Road, the last street before Rockfield Road. They were headed toward the Campus Arboretum. He notified Gayle and Davenport of this development, and the SWAT unit was already getting into place for a shot at the kidnapper and alleged serial killer.

What is Desmond up to? Neil asked himself. He had to put himself in the shoes of his former teaching assistant turned villain. All things considered, Desmond had probably come to realize that this was likely the end of the line. But it was unlikely that he intended to go down without a fight. Or at least without ending things on his own terms.

To Neil, this meant positioning himself away from easy targeting by SWAT members or other authorities. Desmond most likely wanted him as payback for ruining his best-laid plans with Connor Vanasse. And taking Paula's life too would give Desmond the ultimate satisfaction to take with him to the grave.

Neil sucked in a deep breath as he headed for the Campus Arboretum, while hoping to avert a catastrophe that could cost him and Paula their lives.

Not to mention a future together.

PAULA PARKED IN an area that was off Mumbly Drive, the main road to the Campus Arboretum. She was quickly forced out of the car by Desmond at gunpoint and made to move through the woodlands—featuring a plethora of silver maple, black ash and beech trees, various herbaceous plants and a migrant bird sanctuary.

"This is pointless, Desmond," she protested, trying to buy more time. "Give it up. I can protect you from harm, if you hand me your gun and mine. You'll get a fair trial—"

"Yeah, right." He gave a sardonic chuckle. "There's not much defense for suffocating six pretty professors. And, very soon, you can add to that killing a visiting professor with ATF credentials. Oh, and did I forget—a good-looking campus police detective too. Thanks, but I think I'll see what awaits me on the other side after a bit of unfinished business…"

They heard the rustling of trees and crunching of dirt, causing Desmond to instinctively grab Paula from behind and place the gun to her temple. "Come out," he demanded. "Or I'll put a bullet in Detective Lynley's pretty head before you can even think about dropping me."

"All right, all right," said the deep and most familiar voice. Out of the trees came Neil, who had his Glock 47 pistol out and aimed directly at Desmond. "I'm out. You've got me, Desmond. I assume this is what you wanted…?"

"Yeah, sure." Desmond laughed. "I have to admit, Professor Ramirez, you gave me a bit of a start. Thought I had more time to work with in getting my captive here to a more secluded location, while waiting for you."

"You thought wrong." Neil's voice raised an octave. "I'm a profiler, remember? I was able to anticipate your latest moves before you could make them. Now let her go and we can settle this man to man."

Desmond growled like an animal. "You'd like that, wouldn't you?" He tightened his grip on Paula. "She stays right where she is. I suggest you drop your gun, Special Agent Ramirez. Or I'll simply blow the detective's brains out, right here and now. Then you can shoot me to death before the cavalry arrives and take all the credit for downing the Campus Killer. Your call."

It was clear to Paula that Neil had no intention of giving in to Desmond's demands, no matter how tempting, knowing full well that to do so would be signing both their death warrants. On the other hand, she could feel the tension in the killer's body, pressed up against hers. He was a powder keg that was ready to explode at any time. She couldn't let that happen. She wouldn't allow Desmond to call the shots any longer. Not when it literally meant the difference between life and death for all three of them.

For two, at least, she had a better plan of action and survival.

Paula lulled Desmond into a false sense of security by saying meekly, "You win, Desmond. I'm done with this. Go ahead and get it over with and I'll die knowing that Neil took a serial monster off the streets of Rendall Cove..."

As the Campus Killer seemed momentarily confused, using her skills in Krav Maga, Paula caught him off guard by swiftly slamming the back of her head into his face as hard as she could. At the same time that she heard his facial bones fracturing, she pushed the gun away from her head as it fired off one round up into the trees.

Desmond howled like a seriously wounded animal, and his firearm fell harmlessly onto the ground while he put both hands to his face. Whipping around, Paula was taking no chances for a quick recovery by the serial killer—using a self-defense technique to knee him hard in the groin.

While he bowled over in pain, her adrenaline rush was still high, but Paula felt herself being pushed aside. She watched as Neil took over, landing two solid blows to Desmond's head, before the kidnapper and killer fell flat on his bloodied face, knocked out cold. Neil quickly put Desmond's arms behind his back and Paula cuffed him.

"Are you all right?" Neil asked her gingerly, taking her into his protective arms.

She nodded, glancing at Desmond. "I'm a lot better than him," she answered unsympathetically.

"Did he hurt you?"

"Not really." She made a silly face. "Only the pain of knowing he'd managed to get away with it for so long."

"Well, that's over now. Thanks to you." Neil pulled back, so she could see the little grin playing on his mouth as he looked at the still unconscious serial killer. "I didn't realize you had that fighting combo in you. Wow!"

She laughed. "Guess there are still things you need to learn about me."

"I suppose. Where did that come from?"

"A very wise self-defense instructor in Krav Maga," she told him, separating from him as she went over to the fallen foe and reclaimed her SIG Sauer pistol. She put it back into its holster. "Figured the martial arts would come in handy someday. Guess today is that day."

"And very timely, if I say so myself," he said with a laugh.

Paula met his eyes. "Can't argue with you there." She

paused. "Desmond fessed up about everything, including setting up Connor and hoping to get away with it."

"I expected as much." Neil gave a knowing nod. "Guess Desmond was glad, in his own way, to get this off his chest."

She tilted her face and glanced at his former TA. "That he did, though you'd know better than I would about how the psyche of a serial killer works."

Neil regarded her in earnest, and his voice cracked when he uttered, "If I had lost you—"

Paula put a finger to his lips, knowing she felt the same way about losing him. "You didn't," she told him. "And I didn't lose you either, thank goodness."

"True." He took a breath. "But with the thought of that, and before the team comes and takes over, I don't want to wait a moment longer to tell you just how much I love you, Paula."

"Then don't," she teased him.

Neil laughed. "Yeah, I love you, Detective Lynley."

"That works both ways, Agent Ramirez. Very much so." She cupped his cheeks and laid a hearty kiss on Neil's lips, so as to leave no doubt.

Paula only wished that the same could be true for where things went from here, as the criminal investigation that brought them together wound down with the capture of the real Campus Killer, at last.

Epilogue

Members of the Bureau of Alcohol, Tobacco, Firearms and Explosives, Rendall Cove Police Department's Firearms Investigation Unit and the Shays County Sheriff's Department converged on the American foursquare home on Vernon Drive. Parked in the driveway was the silver Lincoln Navigator Reserve registered to alleged gunrunner Craig Eckart, and a blue BMW 228i Gran Coupe registered to known Eckart associate Salvador Alonso, and a red Jeep Wagoneer belonging to ATF agent Vinny Ortiz. The undercover operative had just sent out a text, signaling that the time had come to break up the firearms trafficking network, once and for all. They hoped the raid would send a message that would resonate globally.

Wearing a ballistic vest and armed with his Glock 47 Gen5 MOS 9x19mm pistol, Neil joined his heavily armed law enforcement partners, equipped with arrest and search warrants for the takedown. That included bringing in an officer from Animal Control to handle the potentially aggressive Staffordshire bull terrier that Eckart was known to own. Waiting in the backdrop were crime scene investigators and an ambulance, if needed.

Using fierce determination, overwhelming power

and a battering ram, the front door was forced open and the house inundated with the team, able and ready to handle any resistance. The dog was quickly subdued and removed from the premises. Fanning out to each and every room, arrests were made of three men and two women. The former included Craig Eckart and J. H. Santoro—Ortiz's alias. Ortiz, who put up a good act of appropriate belligerence and outrage over the arrest, was handcuffed along with the other suspects.

"Tell it to the judge," Neil snapped at him believably, while handing him over to an FIU detective.

"I will," Ortiz muttered convincingly, as he was led away without further incident.

Neil watched as Craig Eckart looked shell-shocked at the prospect of his gunrunning business going up in smoke, while facing potentially decades behind bars for his trouble.

When the dust finally settled, along with a treasure trove of detailed information on contraband firearms and ammunition seized with five cell phones and three laptops, the raid uncovered a cache of unlicensed firearms and rounds of ammunition, huge quantities of fentanyl and quantities of methamphetamine and further evidence of criminal activity that Eckhart and his colleagues were engaged in.

FRESH OFF THE successful raid of Craig Eckart's illegal weapons enterprise, Neil was back at Horton Hall, having already mapped out his future where it concerned Paula and a life together, when he was summoned to the office of School of Criminal Justice Director Stafford Geeson.

He walked in to find Geeson standing by a picture window, seemingly deep in thought. Neil imagined that he was wondering how he could have missed the signs of the evil that lurked within his teaching assistant, Desmond Isaac. *Believe me, I'm asking myself the same thing,* Neil thought, but he took solace in knowing that he had figured out Desmond's true character before he was able to successfully pin the murder rap on Connor Vanasse. Not to mention add Paula as another notch on his belt of victims.

"Stafford—" Neil got his attention.

Geeson faced him and forced a grin. "Neil—thanks for coming."

"No problem." He met the director's eyes curiously. "Everything okay?"

"Yeah, I'm fine. The School of Criminal Justice will continue to do its thing in educating and preparing the next generation of people in law enforcement to fight the good fight, in spite of our one giant setback and disappointment in Desmond Isaac."

Neil frowned. "We're all disappointed in him and the horrible choices he made."

"He'll have a lot of time to digest it behind bars," Geeson pointed out with satisfaction in his voice. "Anyway, I didn't ask you to drop by to talk about him." He paused. "Have a seat."

"All right." Neil sat on a blue task chair by the window and watched as Geeson sat nearby. *So, is this where he cans me with my contract nearing an end?* Neil mused. Or the opposite?

After a moment or two, Geeson eyed him squarely and said, "I'm not sure what your plans are, insofar as returning to full-time work as an ATF special agent or another avenue, but during your short tenure here at Addison University, you've become one of the most liked and respected professors in the School of Criminal Justice. Using your expertise to help flush out the Campus Killer—especially when it was one of our own—only enhanced your stature around here." He paused. "What I'm trying to say is that I'd like to offer you a full-time position as an associate professor of criminology—if you're interested...?"

"I'm definitely interested." Neil didn't have to think very long about the offer. Particularly since it was an avenue he would have pursued, had the director not beaten him to it.

"I'm happy to hear that." Geeson's face lit up. "So, are you in...?"

"Yeah." Neil grinned. "I'm in."

"Welcome aboard for the long term, Professor Ramirez." They stood up and shook hands firmly.

Back in his own office, Neil rang his boss at the Grand Rapids ATF field office, Doris Frankenberg, and said in earnest, "We need to talk."

A few minutes later, he was in his car, where Neil got Paula on speakerphone and asked coolly, "Where are you?"

"On my way home," she told him, and he could hear some background noise. "Where are you?"

"Headed to your house," he responded simply. "See you shortly."

"I'll be waiting..."

After disconnecting, Neil couldn't wait to be face-to-face with her. But first, he had a stop to make.

PAULA WAS HAPPY to chill at home, following a workday that included clearing up a few loose ends in the Campus Killer case. There would still be more to come, even with Desmond Isaac's capture and confession. Such as piecing together how he had been able to succeed in his depravity for as long as he had and what could be learned from this for future serial killer investigations by the Department of Police and Public Safety.

But at the moment, Paula admitted that she had butterflies in her stomach knowing Neil was on his way over. She suspected he wanted to talk about their future. Or perhaps his waning time as a visiting professor. For her part, she had decided that as much as she loved her job, it paled in comparison to the love she felt for Neil. She would gladly relocate to his work place if that was what it took for them to be together.

When he knocked on the door, Chloe meowed, as if she'd been anticipating his arrival and welcomed his presence as much as Paula. The cat ran to the door, and Paula followed the Devon rex in her bare feet and opened it, only to see a grinning Neil standing there, holding a dozen long-stemmed red roses.

"What's this?" She batted her eyes demurely.

"For you," he said with a lilt in his voice. "Just a little something I picked up along the way."

Neil handed them to her, and Paula put the roses up to her nose and took in the delightful floral scent. She flashed her teeth at him. "They're lovely," she gushed as they made their way into the great room.

"Not half as lovely as you," he asserted while allowing Chloe to rub against one of his brown Chelsea boots.

"Thank you." She blushed and went into the kitchen to put the roses in water.

When Paula returned to the great room, she could tell that something was on Neil's mind. *Me, I hope*, she told herself, but asked evenly, "So, what's up?" She'd heard that the ATF-led operation against suspected arms trafficker Craig Eckart had been successful. It was a big win for the task force and city of Rendall Cove in curbing the proliferation of illegal weapons across the globe.

After he commented keenly on this, Neil took her hands and looked Paula directly in the eyes and asked casually, "Feel like getting married again?"

Her eyes ballooned at his face. "Is that a proposal?"

"Yeah, it is," he made clear. "I'm in love with you, Paula. You already know how I feel. I think the same is true from your end. So, why not make it official? Be my wife and we can have a great marriage and all that comes with it."

Paula felt the beat of her heart, erratic as it was. This was something she had dreamed of—a second opportunity to find true love. Neil checked every box in that department and then some. There was one other thing to address though, even if it had no bearing on her decision, per se, but was important nevertheless.

"What did you have in mind for us once your visiting professorship stint ends?" She angled her eyes at his curiously. "To be sure, I'm more than ready and willing to relocate to Grand Rapids—or elsewhere, if necessary, to be with you…"

A smile played on Neil's lips as he said nonchalantly, "Actually, about that… I was just offered a full-time position by the director of the SCJ, which I happily accepted.

So, I'm not going anywhere. Not unless you want to leave Rendall Cove. If that's the case, count me in on wherever you want to set up shop. It doesn't matter, as long as we're together."

Paula beamed. "Congrats on the wonderful news in becoming a faculty member and no longer just a visiting professor. I'd love to stay put in this college town in my current position with the Investigative Division of the DPPS—and build a family with you, Neil."

"Are you saying what I think you're saying?" His voice cracked.

Her teeth shone. "Yes, I'm madly in love with you, Professor Neil Ramirez, and would be delighted to become your bride and mother to any children you'd like to have."

"As many kids as we're comfortable with, while being able to balance that with our work lives and quality time as a couple," he told her, his tone genuine.

"Well, all right, then." She chuckled, excited at what was to come for them. "It looks like we're now engaged to be married." Paula knew the engagement ring would come soon enough. Right now, she was more than content simply to have his heart.

"I couldn't be happier," Neil promised, wrapping his arms around her protectively. "But I think it's imperative that we seal the deal with a…"

He pulled them apart just enough for Neil to give her a hearty kiss that left Paula light on her feet and feeling that, in this instance, a single action truly did speak louder than hearing the word.

EIGHT MONTHS LATER on their honeymoon, Neil and Paula Ramirez lounged on beach chairs at the Ka'anapali

Beach Resort on the island of Maui, Hawaii. Wearing sunglasses and floral-print swim trunks while sipping on a lava flow, Neil checked out his wife as she talked on her cell phone with her friend, Josie, the two comparing notes on their Hawaiian experiences.

Paula had on a hot red halter bikini top and matching bottoms, showing off her shapely legs. *She's so hot*, Neil told himself admiringly, as Paula took a sip of her blue curaçao before resuming the conversation. She was even more beautiful as the blushing bride when they tied the knot a month ago, showing off her princess-cut diamond wedding band to everyone she saw. Attendees included Paula's mother, Francine, and Neil's sister, Yancy, along with Gayle Yamasaki, Mike Davenport and Vinny Ortiz, among others.

Neil shifted his gaze to the seemingly endless Pacific Ocean. There were a few gentle waves brushing against the shore and a couple of boats out for some leisure time. Neil thought about the happenings since he and Paula took Desmond Isaac out of commission. They had located Desmond's laptop and cell phone, each of which contained important evidence attesting to his guilt as the Campus Killer.

His full, official confession to six murders, one attempted murder and kidnapping and a few other charges thrown in for good measure landed Desmond Isaac in the Ionia Correctional Facility, or I-Max, in Ionia County, Michigan. There, the maximum-security state prisoner would spend the rest of his life. Thanks in part to Connor Vanasse, whose cooperation in the case against Desmond allowed Vanasse to cop a plea for drug-related offenses, rather than multiple murders, resulting in a few years behind bars.

With Desmond's reign of terror at Addison University over, the campus had returned to being a great place to study. Not to mention a perfect setting for Neil to teach criminology full-time as an associate professor. He had been retained by the Bureau of Alcohol, Tobacco, Firearms and Explosives as a consultant on high-profile cases. Such as the one that brought down arms trafficker Craig Eckart, who, it turned out in an ironic twist, had sold Desmond the Beretta 3032 Tomcat Kale Slushy pistol he used to abduct and try to kill Paula.

Eckart had been convicted on a slew of federal charges and would be spending decades rotting away in the Federal Correctional Institution, Milan, in York Township in Washtenaw County, Michigan. Joining him in FCI Milan was pipe bomber Harold Fujisawa, who would also be incarcerated for a very long time as a convicted domestic terrorist.

But, most of all, Neil was delighted to be a husband to Paula, the gorgeous detective sergeant who continued to make her mark in the school's Investigative Division, in helping to keep it a safe environment for professors and students alike. He was just about to have another sip of his cocktail, when instead Neil felt the softness of Paula's lips on his.

"Just wanted to make sure you were awake," she teased him after the long kiss had ended.

"I am now," he joked, tasting her blue curaçao on his lips.

She laughed. "What do you say we jump into the water for a swim?"

Tempting as that sounded, Neil responded desirously, "I have a much better idea. How about we head back to our room and flex our limbs in a different way?"

"Hmm..." Paula pretended to think about it while flashing her teeth. "Why, that sounds like a fabulous idea, Mr. Ramirez. Works for me."

"I was hoping you'd say that, Mrs. Ramirez." His eyes lit up lovingly as Neil got to his feet, bringing Paula up with him. He kissed her again, allowing it to linger a bit, enjoying this. Then a bit more and a little more after that, before he stopped for now and said definitively, "Let's go."

* * * * *

Look for the final book in R. Barri Flowers's
The Lynleys of Law Enforcement miniseries
when Mississippi Manhunt
goes on sale next month!
And if you missed the previous books in
the series, you can find them wherever
Harlequin Intrigue books are sold:

Special Agent Witness
Christmas Lights Killer
Murder in the Blue Ridge Mountains
Cold Murder in Kolton Lake

HARLEQUIN
Reader Service

Enjoyed your book?

Try the perfect subscription for Romance readers and get more great books like this delivered right to your door.

See why over 10+ million readers have tried Harlequin Reader Service.

Start with a Free Welcome Collection with free books and a gift—valued over $20.

Choose any series in print or ebook. See website for details and order today:

TryReaderService.com/subscriptions

RSBPA24R